He was one hundred percent cowboy...

...and he was shaking his head. "If you like your men principled like your late husband, I'm not going to look so good. I'm sorry I brought him up."

"I'm glad you did. It's silly to pretend he's not here."

"Is he?"

She knew what he meant. She'd thought the land development was the wedge between them; she hadn't realized her late husband might be the true obstacle. "I don't know."

"When two male bison want the same female, they fight it out."

"You're ready to lock horns over me?"

"I know better than to lock horns with a memory. You said it—no one wins a standoff."

Attraction warred with caution, making her heart pound and twist. "So now what?"

"We go back to the way things were. Bring on your persuasion campaign. But know this, darlin'—I won't sell my land. Not now, not ever."

She dragged her gaze away, looking at the awe-inspiring Texas pastures. She knew how he felt about his land. How did she feel about the cowboy?

Allie Pleiter, an award-winning author and RITA® Award finalist, writes both fiction and nonfiction. Her passion for knitting shows up in many of her books and all over her life. Entirely too fond of French macarons and lemon meringue pie, Allie spends her days writing books and avoiding housework. Allie grew up in Connecticut, holds a BS in speech from Northwestern University and lives near Chicago, Illinois.

Books by Allie Pleiter

Love Inspired

Blue Thorn Ranch

The Texas Rancher's Return

Lone Star Cowboy League

A Ranger for the Holidays

Gordon Falls

Falling for the Fireman
The Fireman's Homecoming
The Firefighter's Match
A Heart to Heal
Saved by the Fireman
Small-Town Fireman

Visit the Author Profile page
at Harlequin.com for more titles.

The Texas Rancher's Return

Allie Pleiter

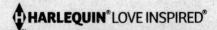

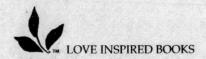

LOVE INSPIRED BOOKS

Recycling programs
for this product may
not exist in your area.

ISBN-13: 978-0-373-04436-8

The Texas Rancher's Return

Copyright © 2016 by Alyse Stanko Pleiter

www.Harlequin.com

Printed in U.S.A.

Live a life worthy of the calling you have received.
—*Ephesians* 4:1

To Charlene

For so many breakfasts,
in the hopes of so many more

Acknowledgments

Special thanks to Beverly Brown
and Donnis Baggett, the owners of the
Lucky B Bison Ranch in Bryan, Texas.
Their hospitality, enthusiasm, generosity in
sharing information and tolerance of
my endless questions have been some of the
great blessings in writing this book.

Chapter One

"Could you please move your buffalo?"

Brooke Calder looked out her car windshield to squint suspiciously at the hairy brown beast currently staring down her hatchback. Buffalo didn't charge, did they? Stampede, maybe, but she wasn't about to get a set of horns impaled in her front grill, was she? She leaned out the driver's-side window and smiled at the cowboy who had just ridden up beside her car.

The tall man tipped his hat with an amused grin and moved his horse closer to the car. "Daisy is a *bison*, ma'am. And she don't always cooperate, so I hope you're not in a hurry."

She was. These days Brooke was always in a hurry.

She applied her sweetest community-relations voice. "As a matter of fact, I am. So if it's not too much trouble, can you please get her off the road?" The bison's human companion looked a bit scruffy around the edges—handsome, but definitely too young and rough-hewn to be one of the shiny-suited ranchers she often had to deal with as a community-relations specialist for DelTex Real Estate Developments. A ranch hand? Foreman, more likely. He sat his horse with a commanding air of power.

He leaned toward her, widening the grin. "I'd like to oblige, but Daisy may not be interested in playing nice today."

Brooke couldn't imagine what days bison chose to play nice. "Is she a wanderer?"

"No, just pregnant. Very. Mamas don't usually stray away from the herd unless they're looking for a quiet place to give birth."

Daisy shifted her weight and gave a low, rumbling moan. Brooke didn't know too many people who'd consider the middle of the road a dandy place for child—*calf*-birth. Buffalo—*bison*, Brooke corrected her thoughts, were supposed to be intelligent animals. She'd never win a strength battle of brute animal vs. compact car, so perhaps diplomacy was the way to go here. She leaned out the window to speak in a direct, friendly address. "Congratulations, Daisy. If you'd be so kind as to move, I want to get home to my little girl, too. I'm sure you understand, so could you give me a couple of feet to ease on by?" The ground on either side of the road was muddy, and Brooke didn't want to chance getting stuck by going off-road in a car definitely not designed for off-roading.

The man pulled his horse up to stand even with the creature, who swung her enormous head to look at him. She had pretty eyes—

huge and chocolate-brown, with a wise kind of character to them. "What do you say, Daisy? Shall we let the lady pass?"

Daisy did not seem inclined to move.

"Please, Daisy?" Brooke couldn't believe she was pleading with a giant wall of brown fur.

"Let's just give her a minute." The rancher adjusted his hat. "So, what brings you all the way out here, ma'am?"

"I just came from a meeting over at Ramble Acres."

That caught his attention. He sidled the horse back to her window while Brooke calculated how much of a late fee she'd incur by picking Audie up past six at day care. Again. "You with DelTex?" His tone made it clear that this would not be a mark in her favor.

"I'm Brooke Calder. I work for Jace Markham in the community-relations department."

A sour expression overtook the man's face. "Jace Markham at DelTex. Huh." The words had a definite edge, and Brooke began to wonder if he'd instruct Daisy to stay put for a week or two.

"Do you know Markham, Mr. ….?"

"Buckton. Gunner Buckton. Junior, that is."

Oh. The possibility of bison horns in her front grill increased considerably. While Brooke wasn't intimately familiar with all the details, she was aware of a file in the office—a thick one, at that—with the Buckton name on it. It wasn't full of fan letters to DelTex, that was for sure. Somehow she'd associated the ranch with Gunner Buckton the senior, but he'd passed a while back, hadn't he? This meant Mr. Markham had been locking horns for the past few months with Gunner Buckton *Junior*, the man currently beside her on horseback.

Buckton's now-scowling demeanor didn't bode well for any assistance getting Daisy to move. He looked more prone to inciting Daisy to charge, if bison did that sort of thing. Then again, on a hot afternoon at eight months pregnant, Brooke had been easy to incite, too. The memory of her late husband calling her "Bronco Brooke" while rubbing her very swollen feet shot into her mind and she swallowed hard. *Be nice to the very pregnant bison, Brooke, and maybe she'll move out of the way.*

Buckton's eyes narrowed under the shadow of his hat. She could almost watch him choose to keep a polite tone as he asked, "What DelTex business brings you onto Blue Thorn land, Ms. Calder?"

Brooke looked down at the pavement below her wheels. "I wasn't aware I was on Blue Thorn land, Mr. Buckton. I'm *next* to it—" she nodded toward the fence just behind him "—but just passing through on my way back into Austin. That is until Daisy decided to play roadblock." She could do without the suspicious glare touching the corner of the man's startling blue eyes.

"She's just looking for some solitude,"

Buckton said, shifting his gaze back and forth between Brooke and Daisy. "She wants a little space to share with the young'un when the time comes."

"Don't we all?" Brooke replied. When was the last time she'd spent an unhurried afternoon with Audie? Suspecting she'd lost her chances with the rancher, Brooke leaned out the window to try again with the bison. "Mama to mama, Daisy, could we hurry things along? I expect we all want to get home to supper."

Daisy actually snorted in reply but didn't move. Brooke began to feel like snorting herself. "Is that bison for yes or no?" At the moment, it looked like bison for *I'll take an hour or so to think it over.*

"I *really* don't want to be late picking up my daughter." She wasn't quite sure if she should address her plea to Buckton or Daisy. Neither seemed all that inclined to listen to her.

Buckton scratched his chin. He was rather

nice-looking for someone not so nice. "Did you try your horn?"

"Of course I did. First thing, but…" The flimsy, near-silly horn was one of the things Brooke hated most about her little car. She demonstrated its cartoonish beep again for the rancher, feeling the color rise to her cheeks. To Brooke's dismay, Daisy lifted one hoof as if investigating whether she'd stepped on a squeaky toy.

Buckton snickered. "I see your point." He tried unsuccessfully to hold back a laugh. "Baby ducks wouldn't get out of the way of that horn."

Brooke didn't have time for this little standoff. She made a show of looking at her watch, then up at the rancher. "I really am in a bit of a time crunch here. Can you think of anything that might get Daisy to move? I'd be obliged."

Buckton looked at her for a long minute, his sky-blue eyes piercing under the shade of his hat brim. Hadn't she read somewhere that all the Bucktons had the same striking turquoise eyes? Was that where the ranch name had come from? Mr. Markham had certainly made his share of jokes about the Blue Thorn being the "Big Thorn" in his side. Brooke offered Buckton a "pretty please" smile and checked her watch again. Audie hated it when she was the last child to be picked up from day care, and her lonely face sitting on the center steps never failed to make Brooke feel like the Worst Parent of the Year.

Buckton seemed to ponder his options for a moment then suddenly wheeled his horse around and shouted, "*Hee-ya*, girl!" at the massive bison. Daisy lifted her nose from its inspection of Brooke's car hood, swung her huge head between horse and car and then unceremoniously lumbered off in the direction of the open gate Brooke saw down the road. Without a single look back, Gunner Buckton followed his beast.

"Well," Brooke said to the empty car, "if

I'd have known *yelling at it* would have worked..." She called out a cheery "Thank you!" as she drove past Buckton while he swung down off the saddle, presumably to shut the gate behind Daisy.

He simply tipped his hat as she drove by, but when she checked her rearview mirror a few seconds later, he was still standing by the gate, staring at her little car as it hummed down the road.

She'd met the legendary Gunner Buckton Junior. Brooke didn't know if that made things better or worse for the troubled relationship between that man and her boss. Right now the only thing she knew for certain was that it made her late.

Gunner shoved his saddle onto its stand in the horse barn tack room with a bit too much force. The action made his foreman, Billy Flatrock, look up from his work, one bushy eyebrow raised in inquiry. "What's up with you?"

"You'll never guess who Daisy introduced me to this afternoon." Gunner took off his gloves and whacked them against his pant leg, raising up a cloud of yellow dust that swirled in the ribbons of slanted gold light coming through the barn windows.

"Daisy making introductions? I know she's good with people but I didn't think she was feeling so friendly now." Billy shook his head as he squinted at one of his tools.

"She's gonna calve early, Billy. I'm sure of it with the way she's behaving."

"Yep. She'll be our first this year," the Native American confirmed.

Gunner watched the sediment—the dust of his land—slowly settle to his boots. It had been a wet spring, but the air had the smell of a long, dry summer. Would a drought play right into DelTex's land-grabbing hands? "Actually, it wasn't much of an introduction. Closer to a standoff, really." It was kind of fun to watch Daisy stare down the pretty little gal from DelTex's offices right there in the middle of the road.

"Sounds more like one of the bulls than Daisy."

Gunner sat down on the nearest of the dozen or so wooden storage lockers that lined the tack room. "She got out again, Billy. Through the northwest fence. We've gotta find a way to keep that gate locked until we can replace it. If she'd have crossed over onto Larkey's land, it wouldn't have ended well."

"We got more than enough creek on our side of the fence. She don't need what's on Larkey's. She'll get stuck in the mud one of these days if she keeps that up. I keep tellin' her she ain't no water buffalo, but I don't think she pays me any mind." Billy was a trusted friend, and one of Gunner's few allies when he had first returned to the Blue Thorn. One of the last few members of the Tonkawa tribe, Billy claimed to have conversations with several of the animals on the ranch and knew so many uncanny things that no one could work up the courage to question his claims. Even the vet was known to ask Billy's opinion now and then on a particular animal's state of mind.

The amusing image of Brooke Calder's baby-blue car came to him again, idling like an impatient toddler in front of Daisy's curious black nose. "Daisy was standing in the middle of the road, blocking this DelTex lady's car from getting by." He didn't buy her "just passing through on my way back from Ramble Acres" story. No matter her pretty looks, Gunner knew the kind of folks who worked for DelTex. There wasn't a one of them who could be trusted.

Billy's bushy gray eyebrows knotted together. "DelTex, huh?"

Gunner picked a bit of grass off his hat as he ran his fingers around the worn rim. "Young. Nice-looking. She works for Jace Markham."

"Markham." Billy spat the word out as if it

tasted bad as he returned one tool to his box and picked up another to inspect. Markham and his DelTex buddies had been trying for a long time to convince Gunner and his family to sell the land surrounding his back creek. "I guess I'm glad Daisy blocked her in the road."

Gunner hadn't minded it too much himself—except for a hint of guilt over what she'd said about needing to pick up her daughter. Had that been the truth? Brooke looked about his age, but he didn't recall seeing a wedding band on her hand. There was definitely one of those child booster things in the backseat of her car, though. "Are they trying some new tactic on us? After all, I've always figured anyone who worked for DelTex ought to look…" He searched for the least mean word, coming up empty. He'd imagined anyone who worked for Jace Markham to look more…*reptilian*.

"Like Daisy?" Billy let out a laugh that quickly dissolved into a cough. The man's long years on the Blue Thorn were catching up with him.

"Yeah, like Daisy."

The older man wheezed his agreement into a bright blue bandanna handkerchief. Everyone at the Blue Thorn carried or wore the blue bandanna—one of Dad's silly traditions no one had the heart to give up, even though the man had been gone over a year now. "Guess that means that Ramble Acres business is starting up again?" Billy commented.

"Hasn't ever stopped, really." Ramble Acres may look like some pretty development on their shiny brochures, but once it got built, Gunner knew what it really meant for Blue Thorn Ranch and many other area properties. Growing housing developments meant ranch land would disappear in the name of condos and shopping centers.

"That's no good." Billy stood up—the creaky process of unfolding his long legs bringing an extended groan from the man.

There weren't many people on the Blue Thorn taller than Gunner. Even though Billy was well into his sixties, he stood six-three. When Gunner was five, he'd believed the stories his dad told him about Billy's dad being from a tribe of giants that rose up out of the creek.

"No, it isn't good. I've told him we're not selling that land around the creek, but they don't seem to listen." No fancy developer was going to buy any piece of his creek.

"It ain't right, I tell you." Billy settled his hat on his head.

"I won't let them have our land or our water." Big words, but even Gunner knew that ranchers hardly ever won such battles—especially against behemoth companies like DelTex.

Billy put a hand to Gunner's shoulder. "It've killed your papa to give up one inch to those idiot developers." Some people thought the upscale residential development going in near the Blue Thorn was a fine idea. Too many ranchers were tired of the hardships of the ranching life and ready to sell, so they welcomed developers with deep pockets like DelTex. Gunner, like his father before him, wasn't ready to sell off any land, but it was getting harder and harder to hold the line.

You can't have my land, no matter how many pretty ladies you send to bat their eyes at me, Gunner challenged them silently in his mind as he pulled the tack room door shut. *It ain't yours to take, ever.*

Chapter Two

"I hate it when you're last." At the tender age of eight, Audie had already mastered a guilt-inducing pout that could turn Brooke's gut to rock in seconds.

She picked up her daughter's backpack, waving goodbye to the after-school day-care worker, who offered a smile that was half sympathy, half judgment. "I hate *being* last, honey." She forced enthusiasm into her voice. "But I have a great story why. Perfect taco-night conversation."

Friday night tacos had been a tradition since Audie was old enough to eat them, and it helped to put the stress of the working week to bed for both of them. While the rest of single parenting often eluded her, Friday Tacos for Two was one of the things Brooke felt she got right. Jim's death two years ago had left them both reeling, and since the Friday Taco Trio that was his idea was no longer an option, Friday Tacos for Two had been one of a hundred reinventions life had forced on them.

"I pick Edie's," Audie announced as she flipped the passenger seat forward and crawled into her booster in the car's tiny backseat. Each Friday, Audie could choose which of the four local taco joints would serve their feast. Audie was never short of opinions on any subject, so Brooke liked to give her opportunities to choose whenever she could. Brooke scanned the shrinking space between Audie's pigtails and the car roof—in another year, she'd need a new car. She needed a new lots of things, which made the well-paying job she'd only recently landed at DelTex such a relief.

"Good choice." Brooke nodded as she twisted the key in the ignition, noting the hesitant hiccup in the car's ignition with a hint of concern.

"So what made you late?"

Brooke gave a silent prayer of thanks that Audie hadn't added "this time." She was late more often than she liked, but she had to hold her own with a lot of DelTex's other staffers, who seemed to have no other commitments in life than Margarita Night at the local roadhouse.

"Oh, this is a good one," Brooke teased, catching Audie's dark brown eyes in the rearview mirror as she pulled out onto the avenue. "But you'll have to tell me about your day first before you get this story over tacos."

Audie shrugged—a gesture so much like her father that Brooke felt a familiar ache of grief rise and push under her ribs. "Nothin' really happened. Melissa's still mad at Luke. Oh, Maria and me got partnered for a science project."

A third-grade science project. Brooke had visions of shoe-box dioramas or poster boards. Given her marketing and presentation skills, Brooke thought this might be one parenting area she could ace. "What about?"

"Native Texan animals."

"Any in particular?"

"We can pick one we like. Of *course* Robbie and Jake chose longhorns, and Steve and Marcus chose bats. Maria and I were thinking about buffalos or armadillos."

Brooke raised an eyebrow. "No kidding! Then you're really gonna want to hear my dinner story. You'll be glad I was late by the time I'm done telling you what happened to me today." *Thanks, Lord.* Brooke shot a sigh of gratitude heavenward as she pulled into Edie's Taco Patio, glad to feel a genuine smile fill her face.

"Why?"

"Oh, no, you don't. You're not getting it out of me before table grace, you sneaky little girl. Come on, let's eat."

Audie scrambled out of the seat the moment the car was turned off, all traces of her former gloom gone, replaced by a wide, expectant grin Brooke felt down to her toes. "Did you squash an armadillo with your car? Is that why you're late?"

Brooke ignored the dig and mimed zipping her lip into silence as she pulled open the restaurant door. If she played her cards right, getting blocked by the giant mama bison wouldn't end up being the disaster she'd beaten herself up for the entire drive to Audie's day care.

"Soooo?" Audie pleaded the minute they were seated with a pair of tacos each, her daughter's eyes wide and brown as a cow's— or was that a bison's?

"Grace first," Brooke countered, gratified that most of the frantic sourness of her 5:55 pickup had evaporated. She bowed her head, but stole a look up for her favorite sight in all the world: Audie's small pink hands folded in prayer, the full brown lashes of her closed eyes lush against rosy cheeks. Was there a sweeter sight this side of heaven? "Dear God, thank You for these tacos and our time together. Thank You for all You provide, and may we always be truly thankful." She waited for Audie's contribution to the prayer, for they each took part in table grace.

"Thank You that Hammie's okay and that Alex doesn't hate Benjamin anymore. In Jesus's name, Amen."

"Something happened to Hammie?" Brooke inquired, wondering what had jeopardized the fate of the class hamster.

Audie took a bite of taco. "Jenna dropped him," she said with her mouth full, earning a *you know better* scowl from Brooke. "Story!" she pleaded after a dramatic display of swallowing, nearly bouncing in her seat with anticipation.

"I met a real buffalo—a *bison*—today. Up close. Her name was Daisy, and she sniffed the hood of my car so close I bet she left nose prints."

"No kidding? A real live bison? Mrs. Cleydon told me that's their real name, not buffalo."

"So you know that already. I didn't—at least not before today." Brooke pointed at Audie. "See, you're already smarter than me on the subject."

"How big was she?"

"Huge. She filled the whole road. Blocked it, even. I had to sit there until her owner came by and nudged her out of the way. That's why I was late—*last*," she corrected, trying to remember that she wasn't technically late and fined unless she showed up after 6:00 p.m. "A mama bison. Well, soon to be—she's going to have a calf soon."

"A baby bison?" Audie's pigtails bobbed. "Are they cute?"

Brooke thought of the massive head with

the enormous brown eyes that stared her down on the road and tried to imagine it miniaturized into baby form. Impressive, maybe, but not cute. Then again, the man who'd ridden to her aid could be called both impressive and cute, if she were inclined to classify, but there were several dozen professional reasons not to pursue that avenue.

"So when I can meet them?"

"The ranchers?" Gunner Buckton didn't look like the kind of man to take a shine to field trips.

"No, silly, the mama bison. That'd make the best report ever—totally better than armadillos. Maria and I would get an A for sure. Please, Mom? Can I?"

Suddenly, this didn't seem like the academic ace in the hole anymore. For all her community-relations skills, Buckton didn't seem likely to cooperate if she came to him with a request for an "up close and personal" with one of his herd. "I don't know."

"I could interview the man who owns her.

I could interview the mama bison. Get my picture with her. That'd be loads better than just looking stuff up on the internet. Maria would just *die* if we could add that to our report."

The eagerness in Audie's eyes made Brooke want to cringe. "He's just someone Mommy met on the road. I don't think he'll say yes."

"I thought you told me sometimes your job was to help people say yes to things."

Brooke suddenly regretted her oversimplified explanation of corporate community relations. "That's true, but maybe not in this case. The rancher and the company I work for are...well, we're sort of in an argument." She could think of no other way to explain real-estate conflicts to an eight-year-old bent on bison interaction. Still, the timing seemed too good to ignore. "Well," she hedged, "we'd have to ask *very* nicely and be okay if he said no."

Audie licked taco sauce off her thumb. "I

could do that. I could tell him it's for school and everything. Could we ask tomorrow? I'd give anything to tell Maria I met a bison for real when we get back on Monday."

Even if he declined, Gunner Buckton at least didn't seem like the kind of man to be mean to an eight-year-old asking to do a school report. Nothing ventured, nothing gained, right? "Okay, honey. But remember, he may say no."

Audie rolled her eyes. "I get that, Mom. You said it already."

"Tell you what—if he does, maybe I can look around online and find another bison rancher." Were there many around? Cattle, yes, but bison? She'd better come up with some truly persuasive tactic when she made that call.

Audie smiled. "You're the best, Mom." She air-kissed Brooke in the way she'd seen two celebrities do on television the other night. Audie was growing up too fast. Still, the shift from "I hate it when you're late" to

"You're the best" was a welcome change on a Friday night. Now all she needed was a small yes from one cooperative bison and her willing owner—*that's not too much to ask, is it, Lord?*

Gunner was draining the last of his Saturday morning coffee when Gran swept into the kitchen with a peculiar expression on her face. She held her cane in one hand and the cordless phone in the other. "Gunner, you have a young lady asking for you on the phone."

Gunner made a split-second mental survey of the young women likely to ring him up before 10:00 a.m. on a Saturday and came up empty. Oh, sure, back in the day the list might have been long, but he wasn't that guy anymore. He certainly couldn't think of any current females who would produce the amusement currently sparkling in Gran's eyes. He wasn't quite sure what was coming when he took the phone. "Buckton here."

"Mr. Buckton?"

Gunner felt his eyes pop at the child's voice. Granny stifled a giggle. When she'd said *young lady*, he sure wasn't thinking *this* young. "Yes?"

The little voice grew serious. "My name is Audrey Calder, and my mom met you and Daisy on the road yesterday."

So Brooke Calder was indeed a mom. This was getting more interesting by the minute. "I remember."

"Well, it just so happens Maria and I want to do a report on bison for our native Texan animals project. Bison are much better than armadillos, don't you think? I'm in the third grade."

Gunner ran one hand down his face. What third grader started a sentence with *it just so happens*?

"Not a big fan of armadillos myself. A report on bison, huh?"

"Your grandma sounds really nice. I told her I wanted to interview Daisy, and she said

I had to ask you. Can I talk to Daisy for my school report?" Then as if it had just occurred to her that no one conversed with a bison—no one except Billy, that was— she added, "Oh, and you, too. Mom told me Daisy's about to be a mommy. Maybe you could tell me more about that."

Well, well, Brooke Calder, seems you belong in Markham's office after all, Gunner thought. What a flawless scheme. He'd promised himself that he'd never let anyone from DelTex so much as pass through the gate onto his ranch—but what kind of lout would say no to a third grader? Had Brooke called, he might have hung up on her. But Gran would have his hide if he was rude to Audrey and turned down a little girl's science project.

Gunner was cornered, and he knew it. Brooke Calder had managed to box him in as neatly as Daisy had blocked the car on the road yesterday. "You're right. Daisy'll calve soon. Maybe real soon." A shred of annoyance at being so manipulated kept him from saying yes right away. And he was ashamed of it immediately. Mean was no real way to act toward a little girl—even if her mama worked for the enemy.

"So you're saying I should come right away? Like today? Are they cute?"

Today? How did this turn into an immediate issue? "Are who cute?"

"Baby bison. Mama said Daisy was huge and scary." At this, Gunner could hear Brooke gasp and shush her daughter on the other end of the line. That made him feel a bit better—served that woman right after putting her daughter on the phone like this.

"Yeah," Gunner stammered, remembering Audrey's original question, "I suppose bison calves are cute. Cuter than their mamas, I guess." He was currently calculating just how much like her bold-as-brass mama little Audrey Calder was. He shot a glance toward Gran, who was giving him a look that

warned "Don't you dare turn that sweet little girl down."

"Okay, you can come," he said, feeling the
invitation settle to the bottom of his stomach like a boulder of imminent regret. "How
about after lunch?"

The squeal that filled the phone made Gunner pull the handset away from his ear and
cringe. It made Gran grin. "Thanks, Mister
Buckton. I'll have the best science report in
the whole class 'cause of this!"

Did she have to sound absolutely adorable?
Ten minutes with Gran and the tyke would
probably have his grandmother talked into
a full-scale ranch tour for the whole class.
The Blue Thorn, overrun with little kids—
the notion made him ill. Gunner pinched
the bridge of his nose and began pacing the
kitchen floor. "We'll do our best to help you
with your report, Audrey."

"Call me Audie. Everyone does. I just said
Audrey to be formal-like when making my
request. After today, we'll be friends."

I highly doubt that, Gunner thought silently, scowling, shutting his eyes and reminding himself this was an innocent little girl who had no way of knowing the inconvenience she was about to cause. He was about to let someone from DelTex onto Blue Thorn land—Dad ought to be turning over in his grave right about now. "We'll see you about 1:30? Check with your mama if that's okay." He hoped that would prevent Brooke from getting on the phone. He wasn't sure he could resist a cutting remark—or six—if he spoke with her directly at the moment.

Confirmation acquired, Audie said an excruciatingly cheerful goodbye, insisting she'd "count the minutes" until 1:30. Gunner hung up the phone and tried to think of every possible reason he had to ride into town this afternoon.

"Oh, no, you don't." Gran narrowed her eyes as she took the handset from him.

"What?"

"I can see you conniving ways to get out

of being here when they arrive. I can read you like you have a neon sign blinking over your head, son." She put the phone down on the table. "If you're the head of Blue Thorn, you host its guests."

The head of Blue Thorn. Every day he felt what was asked of him as the head of Blue Thorn Ranch. The weight of proving himself beyond his rebellious past, the pressure to keep the ranch alive and thriving and in the family. It all kept him up nights. Gran had said she was on his side, had begged him to come home and take things over, but he could tell she was still hanging on to a bit of reserve—that she wasn't totally convinced he could handle the job. He deserved that doubt.

Gunner retreated to the coffeepot. "Gran, do you have any idea who that was?"

"It was a sweet little girl doing a third-grade report on native Texan animals. Finally, a child who cares to do schoolwork beyond looking things up on a computer!

You ought to be ashamed of yourself, trying to dodge her the way you were thinking."

"The person who ought to be ashamed is that darling little girl's mother. Brooke Calder works for Markham. At DelTex. I met her yesterday when Daisy got out and blocked her car back on the west road. DelTex is..."

Gran waved a hand in Gunner's face. "I know very well what DelTex is. I hardly think you can put a stubborn bison down to corporate maneuvers. Or a third-grade girl, for that matter."

"That third-grade girl's mama put her up to this."

"Her mama fixed it so that her teacher assigned a report on native species and talked her into choosing bison and opened the northwest gate so Daisy walked out onto the road in front of her car?" Gran crossed her arms over her chest and got that look on her face, that guilt-inducing "what's gotten into you?" stare of which Adele Buckton was a master. "*That's* what you think?"

"Could be." It wasn't as far-fetched as Gran made it sound. Those big development companies would probably try anything to get what they wanted. How many times had gifts arrived at the house or some oh-so-friendly DelTex exec tried to invite himself onto the ranch in the name of "opening a dialogue"? What was to stop them from finding someone who fit his ideal of an attractive woman and sending her out onto his west road? Brooke Calder would probably earn herself a raise for conniving her way onto Blue Thorn land. "You know those people from DelTex have tried all kinds of ways to get their boots on our acreage. This could just be one more. There's an awful lot of money at stake here, Gran."

Gran didn't reply. Instead, she walked over to the cabinet and began to pull out cookie sheets. "What are you doing?" he balked, swallowing the urge to snatch the flat pans from her hands. This wasn't a social call; this was likely a spy mission.

"What does it look like I'm doing?" Gran said, eying him. "We have a child coming to the ranch. I'm baking some cookies."

Gunner started to formulate a long list of reasons why that was a whopping bad idea, but the look from his grandmother silenced him. No matter what the land deed now said, Gran was still the final word on things at the Blue Thorn. If she could read him as well as she claimed, then Gran already knew what he thought of her plans to ply the Calders with cookies. His opinion on hospitality clearly didn't matter, for she began to hum "There'll Be Peace in the Valley" as she walked into the pantry for ingredients.

An earthquake. That ought to do it. Just send a small earthquake about 1:00 p.m., Lord, so I can call this whole circus to a halt. Gunner settled his hat on his head, muttering about pushy little girls and stubborn old women. *Tornado, thunderstorm—I ain't picky, Lord. Just get me out of this.*

Chapter Three

"Why do they call it the Blue Thorn Ranch?" Audie piped up from the backseat as Brooke pulled her little car up to the gate that marked the ranch's entrance. A tall framework of timbers with *BT* at the center stood over a metal gate that joined two stretches of sturdy metal fencing.

"Every member of the Buckton family has bright blue eyes," Brooke answered. "But I don't know about the thorn part—we'll have to ask." Brooke punched a button on the keypad mounted by the drive, announced herself and the gates slid open along the fence line.

A wide-open landscape lay before them, mounds of grass stretching between clusters of trees. Ahead and to the left, the stone house and a series of outbuildings and barns formed the family compound.

"Look." Brooke pointed to three bison enjoying the shade of a large tree.

"I see them!" Audie cheered. "Wow, they are big."

Audie began scribbling in a small notebook, a tiny pink-hued reporter hungry for her story. Even if she had her reservations, Brooke couldn't have denied her daughter this field trip for all the world. Besides, she reasoned with herself, if Buckton was really as grumpy as her earlier encounter led her to believe, at least the grandmother sounded friendly. Adele Buckton was something of a legend in these parts, one of the old-school ranching families with ties to the land that went back something like four generations. In its heyday, Blue Thorn Ranch had been twice its current size and home to some of the state's prize cattle. Adele Buckton's social and philanthropic standing still cast a shadow that was long and wide, even in the woman's advancing years.

The ranch clearly had seen better days, with some of its former grandeur showing signs of wear and tear, but everything was solidly durable and clearly built to last. Some ranches were all about the flash—big showy things with massive houses to match. This place seemed... *Authentic* was the word that came to mind. Sturdy, sensible, determined to stick out the tough times—that was how the place felt as Brooke turned her car up the path toward the house. She looked forward to meeting Adele Buckton.

"I hope Daisy's feeling friendly today," Audie said, reaching into her pink gingham backpack. "I brought her some Goldfish just in case she's hungry." She produced a baggie of the snack crackers, holding it high so Brooke could see it in the rearview mirror.

Brooke pictured the reaction that would

get from Buckton—and it wasn't a charmed smile. "I'm not so sure bison go for Goldfish, honey. Maybe your first question to Mr. Buckton should be to ask what she likes to eat."

"Oh, that's a good one." Audie scribbled a note to herself, tongue sticking out in eight-year-old journalistic integrity. "But it's only three index cards and a diorama, so I don't think I'll need to know much."

The main house was made of tan stone, wrapped with a huge front porch stretching on either side of a big front door. Dormer windows peeked from the second story, and a pair of ancient trees threw dappled shadows onto the front lawn. A picnic table was set with a blue gingham tablecloth and a tin pitcher of wildflowers. The place gave off all the welcome Gunner's tone had not.

This visit was a risk, but Brooke couldn't ever resist a chance to indulge Audie's curiosity. Her daughter's inquisitive nature and bold personality were so very much like her daddy's that it never failed to raise a lump in Brooke's throat. So what if it meant pressing a favor from a grump like Gunner Buckton?

He came out onto the house's wide front porch, his steps the lazy saunter Brooke associated with all Texas cowboys. A big man, he seemed to tower over his grandmother as she came out beside him, leaning heavily on a blond wood cane with a silver handle.

Getting out of the car, Brooke took the walk up to the porch to take in the man she'd only briefly met yesterday. Gunner's bright blue eyes were just like the older woman's, now that she could clearly see his face rather than squinting up at him as she had yesterday. Mr. Markham had indeed told her about the family trait of turquoise eyes— all the Buckton children and grandchildren had them. The grandmother's were warm, friendly and sparkling. Gunner's were cool, clear and intense. The kind of eyes you couldn't stop looking at even though they made you uneasy.

As they reached the porch, Brooke found herself meeting the man's gaze with a friendly "let's just all try to get along" expression.

"Afternoon," he said in a dry tone that translated roughly to *I know that you know that I don't want to do this.*

Audie, as she always did, plowed full speed ahead. "Hi there. I'm Audie Calder, and I'm here to interview Daisy." She waltzed herself right up the pair of low stairs to Mrs. Buckton—smart choice, Brooke mused to herself—and extended a hand.

"And so you are." Adele Buckton's face broke into a broad smile. "I am so very pleased to meet you, young lady. I like a gal who goes at her research with gusto."

Brooke walked up to Gunner and said quietly, "Thanks for this, but I do remember you saying Daisy could be irritable. Are you sure this will be okay?"

Gunner pushed his hat back on his head. "For any other animal I'd say maybe it would be a problem. We do have plenty of bison who don't much take to folks. Only, I think Daisy will be okay. And whatever questions Daisy fails to answer—" his eyes took on just a sliver of a cordiality "—Gran and I can fill in the blanks."

"Can I get my picture with her? For the report?" Audie asked.

"I think we can manage that," Mrs. Buckton replied. "And when we're done, you just happened to come on a day when I made cookies."

Gunner raised one eyebrow in a suspicious glance at his grandmother that told Brooke just how much of a "coincidence" that really was.

"Thank you," Brooke offered again, meaning it. "I know you're busy and…"

"Nothin' to it." Gunner cut her off. "We're all about community awareness out here." The words sounded recited, as if he didn't really mean them.

"Really?" she replied. "I didn't take you as the kind to welcome visitors."

"I'm not the kind to welcome DelTex, if that's what you mean."

Brooke stood as tall as she could. "I'm not here from DelTex, Mr. Buckton. I'm just a mom with a little girl who wants to do a school report."

Gunner pushed out a breath. "Well, in that case, more people need to understand how important the bison are and value them. The bison—and all of us—need the land to thrive. That's something people need to understand."

"Especially third graders," Audie offered.

"And maybe a few big companies I could name," Gunner added in low tones.

Brooke squared her shoulders, trying not to feel small against the man's broad stance. Having met the grandmother, she noted his features took on an odd duality—so like Mrs. Buckton's and yet with such a different attitude. "How about," she said as quietly as she could, "we agree to leave the politics out of this and just let a little girl write a report?"

He shot her a dubious look, crossing his lean arms over his broad chest as Mrs. Buckton took Audie's hand and they stepped down off the porch to walk toward a series of outbuildings. "Is that even possible?" he said the moment the pair was out of earshot.

"Do you really think I set this up as some kind of stunt for work? That I'd use my own daughter to weasel my way onto your land?"

His resulting expression told her that was *exactly* what Gunner Buckton thought. "You work for DelTex."

"Look, your family may have a file inches thick and a long, *thorny*—" she used the word on purpose "—history with my boss, but I assure you, I haven't studied it. That's not even my department, and at this moment it's definitely not my concern. This is about Mrs. Cleydon's third-grade class and nothing else. If you want to blame someone for setting the whole thing in motion, blame Daisy."

"Daisy did what bison do. You're the one who sicced your daughter on my grandma."

Brooke put her hand to her forehead. "She said she needed to learn about buffalo and I'd run into a buffalo...*bison*," she corrected when his eyes narrowed, "just hours earlier. Any parent would have done the same thing."

"Would any parent have let her daughter do the asking so that I'd look like a heel if I said no?"

He had her there. Brooke knew letting Audie make the call worked in her favor. But the truth was Audie was fearless and wanted to make the call. Brooke hadn't talked Audie into anything, but she was guilty of knowing that putting Audie on the phone increased her chances of success. Really, was that so awful if it made today's visit possible?

An argument wouldn't help Audie get her interview, so Brooke squelched her frustration at Gunner and let out a long, slow exhale. "Are you going to let Audie meet Daisy? Because if you're not, then I think it's best I go get her now. But," she added with an effort to keep the edge out of her voice, "I'd really appreciate if you would."

Gunner exhaled himself, although it sounded far too much like a hiss through his teeth. "No, I'll do it. I'd never hear the end of it from Gran if I didn't." He turned to look at her. "I have your word this isn't a setup?"

It was common knowledge that there was no love lost between the Bucktons and Mr. Markham, but it was a little chilling to see how deep the enmity ran. Brooke wasn't fool enough to miss that her boss had his share of critics—every successful man did—but she couldn't shake the way this man's glare settled in the pit of her stomach. "I promise you this is just what it seems—a little girl doing a project for school. One she's really excited about."

Brooke lowered her voice and swallowed her pride. "Since my husband died, things have been a bit on the tight side, and I don't get to pull off many amazing-mom moments. I'd be grateful if we could make this one stick."

A squeal, followed by peals of little-girl-and-old-lady laughter, came from the barn. "Okay," Gunner said. He gave her a look just a few notches softer than his previous glare. "For science and all."

"For science," she echoed as they stepped off the porch in unison. *And not-so-amazing single moms everywhere*, she added silently.

Audie looked shocked once they turned the corner to the small fenced-in yard where Daisy was currently being held to keep her wandering tendencies in check. "Mr. Buckton, she's peeling!"

Gunner had to laugh at that. Daisy's coat was sloughing off in big batches, but he'd never thought of it as *peeling* before. "Well, actually, she's just losing her winter coat. It's called molting."

"Does it hurt?"

"I suppose it itches. She and the other bison rub up against things to help the old hair come off."

Audie cocked her head to one side, braids bobbing. "Doesn't she need her hair?"

"Yes, but not *that* hair. It's too thick for spring." Okay, so maybe he was enjoying this a tiny bit. Still, he wasn't going to give Brooke Calder the satisfaction of letting it show. He pointed to Daisy as she stood on the far side of the pen. "Daisy has lots of different kinds of hair on her body, which she uses in lots of different ways." Audie stood on the fence rails, her tiny shoulders coming up to Gunner's chest as he pointed out parts of the animal. "The big long eyelashes keep the dust out of her eyes so she can see. And even though she's molting out of her winter layer now, she still has her undercoat— that's the thick fuzzy part underneath that keeps her cool in the summer and warm in the winter."

Audie turned to look at Gunner, wobbling enough on the fence to make Brooke send a protective arm out around her daughter. As she stood on Audie's other side, Gunner noticed that Brooke wasn't much taller than her boosted-up daughter. She might barely meet his shoulder if she stood on tiptoe. Her hair was a creamy honey-blond—much lighter than the dark brown of her daughter's braids, but they looked a lot alike. Except for the eyes—the eyes were totally different. Audie had big brown eyes, whereas Brooke's were a compelling hazel-green. If DelTex had hand-picked her to appeal to him, they'd done their homework. She wasn't one of those fussy, bottle-blonde women many men liked; he preferred her down-home, sensible kind of cute. Had he met her under other circum-stances, if she worked anywhere but where she worked, he would definitely have taken an interest. As it was, cute enemies were still enemies. And kids? Not really his thing.

"Do you ever have to cut her hair to get it out of her way?" Audie's wide eyes brought his attention back to the lesson at hand.

"No. Even when she isn't molting, she rubs up against trees and even some special brushes we set out. So it's more like she combs it out herself. She needs her coat— we wouldn't want to take it away from her. But the parts she's done with can be used in plenty of different ways. The long beard hairs under her chin? Fishermen tell me they make the best flies for fishing. And some people make yarn from the hair she sheds." He was glad Audie kept asking about the fur. It was a safer topic than…

"Mackenzie's Diner by our house sells bison burgers." Audie wrinkled up her nose in thought as she ventured onto the one topic Gunner had hoped to avoid.

He felt his stomach drop a few inches and caught Brooke's panicked eyes over her daughter's head. He shot a look to Gran, who didn't seem at all inclined to take this one for him. This was why he didn't do field trips. There was no safe way to explain slaughter—even carefully humane slaughter—to someone in pigtails with a pink gingham backpack. He ran a hand over his chin, scrambling for an answer. "Yes, people eat bison meat." He dearly hoped the simple truth would settle the matter, but he highly doubted Brooke Calder's superinquisitive daughter would let it go at that.

She didn't. "Do you?"

It was dumb to think the subject wouldn't come up—most people in this small town of Martins Gap knew Blue Thorn for the quality of its meat. If he did his job right, all of Austin would know soon, as well. There seemed no point in lying. "I do. It's very tasty."

"And it's all kind of good for you, too." *Now* Gran piped up. *Thanks for all the help here, Gran.* "Have you ever tasted it?"

"No. But I've seen chickens and I eat them. Seen cows and eaten them, too. I had beef tacos last night. Every Friday's Tacos for Two night."

Brooke went pink, and Gunner tried unsuccessfully to swallow his laugh. "No foolin'?" Then, because it felt safe to do so, he added, "We're not fixing to eat Daisy, if that's what you're asking."

"We're careful to take care of the mamas and their babies here," Gran added.

That seemed to settle the subject to Audie's satisfaction. "That's good," the little girl said, and Gunner felt the same relief he could see in Brooke's eyes.

"Bison have families, just like people," Gran went on. "We keep family groups together because it makes the bison happy."

"Where's your list of questions for Daisy?" Brooke asked, clearly eager to change the subject.

"Right here." Audie popped down off the fence and zipped open her backpack to pull out a purple glitter notebook. Really, it was hard to get more "little girl" than a purple glitter notebook—except for the pink polka-dot pencil that emerged from the backpack immediately behind the notebook. Gunner suppressed a cringe worthy of a third-grade boy's distaste for "cooties."

"Can I talk to her? Up close?"

More parental land mines. Brooke seemed to be remembering that Daisy was as large as her car, her hand going reflexively to Audie's shoulder. There wasn't much to worry about, provided Audie listened to directions, but even Gunner's limited experience with youngsters told him "listening to directions" didn't top the list of their skill sets. He sent Brooke a "let me handle this" glance over Audie's head just before squatting down in front of the girl. "Well, now, that depends on you." He made his voice friendly but serious. "Daisy's a very big animal. And she's easily upset, being so close to her time and all. She's not like a dog or a cat or even a horse who's really used to folks being around. Can you understand that?"

Audie nodded just as seriously. "Oh, I can. Yessir." Brooke looked slightly less alarmed, and Gran smiled.

"She may not be in much of a mood to chat, so I've asked my friend Billy to come along. Daisy does most of her talking to Billy." He felt ridiculous saying that, all the more because it was true as far as he knew. "He can help with the answers you can't get from Daisy or me or Gran."

This didn't seem to faze Audie at all. "Three people and a bison. This'll be the best report ever."

Gunner wasn't sure how true that was, but at least this "interview" wasn't feeling like the intolerable chore he'd imagined it to be this morning. "We'll do our best." He straightened back up as he saw Billy bringing Daisy closer. No matter what, Gunner would keep a sturdy fence between the thousand-pound beast and the bitty Calder women. As a bottle-raised orphan whose parents had been humans rather than bison, Daisy was by far one of the friendliest bison the Blue Thorn had ever seen—but animals were still animals.

Coming up to the fence, Daisy gave an enormous snort, swiveling her huge head around to consider her small pink visitor. "Billy Flatrock, Daisy," Gunner began the introduction even though it felt silly, "this here's Audie." He caught Brooke's eye for a fraction of a second. "Daisy already met Mrs. Calder yesterday."

"Hi, Daisy!" Audie said brightly, much less intimidated by the wall of brown fur in front of her than her mother had been the day before. As a matter of fact, Brooke still looked a bit wary. "Mom," Audie whispered loudly, elbowing her mother, "say hi."

Brooke straightened up. "Hello, Mr. Flatrock. Hello, Daisy. Congratulations to Daisy on being a mama soon."

"Yep. That's really exciting." Audie poised

her thick pink pencil over her notebook like a candy-coated junior reporter. "Tell me, Daisy, do you want a boy or a girl baby bison?"

To Gunner's amazement, Daisy actually looked as if she was considering the question before she gave a series of low, rolling grunts. Gunner felt as though he was losing control of the situation with every passing minute.

Audie looked right at Billy and in all seriousness asked, "What'd she say?"

Billy took the whole thing right in stride. "Daisy had a girl bison last year, so she wants a boy this time." When Gunner raised an "aren't you taking this a bit far?" eyebrow, Billy added, "I think."

All the adults waited while Audie carefully wrote "baby boy" on her notepad. The girl then proceeded to work her way through a set of ten questions—some crazy, others downright thoughtful for someone so young. From Gran's expression, she appeared to be growing fonder of Brooke and Audie every second. When Audie complimented Daisy on the soft new coat coming out from under the old one and her "be-yu-ti-ful" eyes, Gunner felt the cuteness factor tip over his toleration level. *Suddenly, I'm a bison's publicist.* He could almost hear his father's amused laughter echoing out across the ranch. No telling what would happen if any of the other ranch owners got even a whiff of this.

Still, the kid was so excited, he couldn't be entirely annoyed, even if the whole thing took twice as long as he'd planned. Brooke Calder looked at him as if he was some kind of hero, instead of just being a busy rancher who'd just gotten lassoed into the strangest social call of the year.

When Audie finally got the "reply" to her final question, Gran pronounced it time for cookies and lemonade on the lawn. He'd clean forgotten about Gran's social plans, and watched helplessly as another work hour of his afternoon evaporated before his eyes.

He envied Billy as the man walked free and clear into the barn. The foreman offered him a smug smile, glad to be escaping the ladies' tea party Gunner now was forced to endure.

He gave Daisy a long last look as he stepped onto the porch behind the chattering females, and even the bison seemed to enjoy his predicament. "See what I started?" the big brown eyes seemed to say.

Thanks for that, Gunner thought as he tucked his long legs under the picnic table and reached for a cookie.

Chapter Four

Jace Markham leaned back in his chair Monday morning, the Austin sunshine pouring through the many windows of his corner office at DelTex's corporate headquarters. He smiled. "Brooke Calder, I underestimated you."

Brooke looked up from her agenda notes. "How's that?"

"I've been trying to work my way into Adele Buckton's good graces for years now, and you did it in four months."

Brooke felt a little band of annoyance stretch under her stomach. DelTex offices weren't exactly small, and Austin was a big city—how had word of her visit to Blue Thorn traveled so fast? "It wasn't a professional visit, Mr. Markham."

Mr. Markham chuckled as he unbuttoned his suit jacket. "Oh, no, I heard the bit about the book report. Brilliant."

"Science project. And it really wasn't anything more than that. I ran into one of their bison on my way back from picking up files at the Ramble Acres site."

Mr. Markham's eyes popped. "You ran over one of their herd?"

"No." Brooke winced at the poor choice of words. "I met Daisy as she blocked my way across the road. Gunner Buckton came by and helped get the bison out of the road so I could get home."

The big man chuckled. "Well, that's a bit easier to understand. I couldn't quite see how you turned roadkill into a social call." He leaned forward. "I take it you received a chilly reception?"

"At first. And most definitely from Gunner. Gunner Junior, that is. He iced over the minute he worked out who I was. Then Audie decided to do her native Texan animals report on bison, and I didn't see how I could let an opportunity like that get away."

Mr. Markham raised an eyebrow. Brooke meant an opportunity for hands-on learning for her daughter, but clearly her boss had other interpretations.

"I had Audie call and ask to see the bison because I was sure he'd refuse me," she continued. "Only, Audie reached Adele first, and Mrs. Buckton warmed to the idea of a visit right away—maybe because she didn't yet know where I worked." Brooke shifted her weight. "They don't think very highly of DelTex. They think Ramble Acres will eventually spread to take their land."

The vice president took off his reading glasses. "Oh, that's no news to me. These ranchers are passionate about their land. Most times that's a good thing. Only, some-

times the public good clashes with that stubbornness, and forward-thinking developers
like ourselves have to make unpopular proposals."

"I know." It was one of the reasons Brooke
had a job—sometimes the public needed education, or awareness, or just flat-out convincing that a development was good for
everyone. Part of what she did at DelTex was
to help local folks see past the temporary in-
conveniences of development and embrace
the long-term advantages. Or in cases like
Ramble Acres, see why some private land
was going to be needed to make way for
the infrastructure to support a large-scale
project.

"And that's why we pull in the local lead-
ers to get those proposals green-lighted. You
know the song—everybody wants a highway, so long as it doesn't cross the back forty
that's been in their family for three generations."

Brooke was indeed familiar with the conflict. She'd spent the past four months fine-tuning presentations for DelTex execs and the involved local politicians. Infrastructure almost always needed land, and that was a surefire recipe for public conflict. "It did end well, if that's what you're asking. Audie had a wonderful time, and Adele is just like I imagined her."

"Adele Buckton is a grand, gracious lady. She and Gunner Senior became fixtures in this part of Texas back when I was younger than you." Mr. Markham folded his hands on his dark marble desktop. "I've always thought Adele would see reason much faster than Gunner Junior. That boy has his dad-dy's stubborn streak, that's for sure."

Brooke thought of the tall, commanding rancher she'd spent time with and found *that boy* nowhere near a fitting term. "I know the basics of the project, Mr. Markham, but what exactly is it you want from the Bucktons?"

Mr. Markham stood up and motioned for Brooke to join him in front of the large map that took up most of one office wall. He ran a finger down the highway Brooke had traveled on Friday afternoon, the one where she'd met Daisy. "This is Buckton's place." He tapped the finger on the east side of the highway. "Over here is Paul Larkey's ranch," he continued, shifting his finger to the west side. "And here is Ramble Acres." He pointed to the site of Brooke's meeting, a large, upscale housing venture getting ready to go up northeast of both ranches. It was a multimillion-dollar development, sure to be the jewel in the DelTex crown once completed. Mr. Markham had been working on the project—which hadn't even broken ground yet—for the better part of four years. Brooke's presentation had dozens of bullet points about its potential positive impact on property tax revenues, schools and local commerce. In fact, the push to break ground on Ramble Acres was the main reason she'd been hired.

Mr. Markham ran his fingers down a thin

blue ribbon running across all three properties. "Here is what all the fuss is about. We need access to this water system as part of the Ramble Acres drainage plan—storm-water runoff, that sort of thing. Nothing chemical or even remotely detrimental to the land, just the ability to utilize the waterway. But it'll swell that creek with all that water once everything's up and running, so we need Buckton to sell us the creek and the land around it."

"And he won't?" The answer to that question was pretty clear.

"Not yet. He's not budging, even though he's got two other water sources on his ranch, and I know he could use the money. His neighbor Larkey has already said he'd sell. Only, because Larkey is downstream of Buckton, his yes doesn't do us any of good without Buckton's land."

"Sounds like a standoff." She could easily see that happening, given the personalities involved.

Mr. Marhkam pushed out a breath. "When Gunner Senior died, I thought maybe we could get through to Adele. She's the kind of woman who can grasp the bigger picture, and quite honestly, I wasn't even sure she'd keep the ranch. It would have been too much for her to run alone, and all her grandkids had scattered."

Now the pieces were fitting together. "And then Gunner Junior showed up?"

Mr. Markham picked his finger up off the map to point it at Brooke. "He's convinced I'm out to steal his land—all of it, not just the sliver we need—and there's been no convincing him otherwise." The businessman looked pointedly at Brooke. "Until now, maybe. I take the fact that he let you onto the ranch as a good sign. I hope you realize you are in a unique position to do a lot of good here."

He wasn't wrong in his thinking. Brooke knew that many conflicts of this nature were best solved by a series of face-to-face meetings. Arranging such meetings was a large part of what she did best for DelTex. Ideas and corporations never solved problems as well as people sitting down and talking to each other. Only such sit-downs were often hard to accomplish when one—or both—of the parties dug in their heels, the way the Bucktons had done.

"I'd like to help, sir, but have you met that man?" She shrugged, remembering Gunner's glaring eyes. "I doubt I can convince him of anything."

"Oh, don't doubt yourself. You've capitalized on a bit of good fortune and done what I haven't been able to do—gotten a conversation *started*. That's always the first step. I know you know how these things work—relationships first, agreements later." He put a hand on her shoulder, walking them back to his desk. "Do you think you can take the open door you managed to get and crack it open a tiny bit farther? Do whatever you think will keep the lines of communication open—with either Gunner or Adele. Use whatever budget or resources you need, and fend some of the grunt work off to other staffers if you need to free up your time. Help us reach this goal, Brooke, and you'll have proven yourself an invaluable asset to DelTex."

Up until this morning, Brooke hadn't felt very important at DelTex—just another junior staff member trying to make a name for herself. Now Jace Markham was looking at her as if she had the makings of a key player. His regard kindled a glow of satisfaction Brooke hadn't felt in a long time.

In the two years since Jim's death, Brooke had always felt as though she was just getting by, just eking out an existence. Maybe this year would be the time she'd finally start going somewhere, start setting a real career in motion, become the parent and provider that Audie needed her to be. Was it so far-fetched a notion that God sent Daisy into the road that day to launch a chain of events that might make a real difference in her life? In Audie's? In the whole county by way of Ramble Acres? "Absolutely, boss," she said, picking up her folders. "I'm ready to take on this challenge and show you what I've got."

"Gunner, honey, come in here and look at this!"

Gunner pushed his chair away from his desk—piled high this Wednesday morning with paperwork—and headed into the kitchen. There he found Gran at the computer he'd hooked up for her earlier this year. "Did you crash the hard drive again, Gran?"

Gran pulled off her reading glasses to frown at Gunner. "I did no such thing. I'm reading my email."

Gran had asked for the computer so she could keep up with Gunner's three younger siblings. Most days it was a good thing that Gran regularly corresponded with Gunner's sisters, Ellie and Tess, and Tess's twin brother, Luke. Other days, it just sent new reasons for everyone to stick their nose in his business, thanks to Gran's incessant "updates." *I suppose I ought to be glad she hasn't learned to text on a smartphone yet,* Gunner told himself as he peered at the computer screen.

"What is that?"

Gran *pshawed* at him and swatted his shoulder. "It's a drawing of Daisy. Anyone could see that."

Gunner squinted at the brown blob and noticed it had horns and feet. And a wide cartoon smile with pink hearts around its head. "Never seen a smile like that on our Daisy."

"You'd think you were never eight the way you talk. I changed your diapers, cowboy. Don't you ever forget it." Gran touched the screen. "This is a thank-you picture from Audie."

Brooke Calder now had their email addresses? That woman was even slicker than he'd thought.

"I gave Audie my email address when she

was here so she could get in touch if she had more questions. I like that girl's gumption. She had her mother send over this picture this afternoon." She pointed to the little girl in the drawing, who had a cartoon-style dialogue balloon over her head, reading "Thank You, Blue Thorn!" in scrawling third-grade letters. With the period on the exclamation mark made from a blue heart bearing a smiley face. "At least some young people today still remember their manners. And look, she even drew you."

Gran scrolled the screen and pointed to a tall figure wearing a cowboy hat—and a frown. The figure representing Gran was all smiles, holding a cane in one hand and a plate of cookies in the other. "Mom" and "Me" looked happy, too, with Brooke's curls depicted as a halo of squiggly yellow lines.

"She's got you pegged, I'll give her that." Gran chuckled.

"I was nice to her," Gunner protested. "I didn't frown...did I?"

Gran looked up at him. "You didn't smile, either. You mostly looked as if the whole thing hurt like a toothache." She put a hand on Gunner's shoulder. "You went from wild child to serious man. I think you ought to settle yourself somewhere in between, don't you?"

"This serious man has serious work to do. I can't go around playing host to field trips."

"Oh, then you're in trouble now." Gran pursed her lips and then scrolled up to the email that topped the drawing. "Audie's teacher is asking if the class can come visit."

The email included a message thanking Gunner, Gran and Billy for their hospitality and the contact information for Audie's teacher, saying a Mrs. Cleydon was very interested in bringing the class out for a visit.

He pinched the bridge of his nose where a headache was just now starting. "I knew this would happen."

Gran got that look in her eyes. The relentless one Gunner knew all too well. "You are going to say yes. I'm going to write her back right now and tell her we'd be delighted to host the class for an afternoon."

Gunner crossed his arms over his chest. "Didn't you say if I'm head of Blue Thorn I have to do the inviting?"

"Yes. The invitation should absolutely come from you." Gran put her fingers on the keyboard. "Show me how to forward the email and you can reply."

"I don't want to be exchanging emails with Brooke Calder."

"Really, though, wouldn't you be exchanging emails with Audie and her teacher?"

"Through Brooke. I tell you, Gran, that woman is up to no good."

She pointed to the frowning Gunner in Audie's drawing. "That's just your grumpy side talking. She seemed very nice to me. Sweet, even. I give a lot of credit to a young widow like her making her way in the world."

Gran's talent for getting everyone's life

story out of them in twenty minutes or less could be a real annoyance. "Gran…"

"You should help her. You should let those children come see how the ranch works. I've heard you go on and on about conservation and preservation. Well, here's a chance to share those ideas with the next generation. Show these young'uns why they need to care about bison and land and ranches. Show them firsthand, not on that silly Yube-Tube."

"*YouTube*, Gran. And as for conservation and preservation, have you forgotten Brooke works for DelTex? The Ramble Acres company that wants to shave off the back of our property so they can build a shopping mall?"

"Since when can't you be nice to people you disagree with? It's what's wrong with the world, I tell you. That woman has to make a living somewhere—it's not her fault, nor is it Audie's, that her employer happens to be DelTex."

His grandmother's face took on the legendary Buckton stubbornness, a narrow-eyed

I will not back down set of features Gunner knew spelled his surrender.

"You'd better bake a lot of cookies."

She smiled. "Actually, I was thinking brownies. And ice cream. A regular ice-cream social out on the lawn."

Two dozen sticky, squirmy, sugared-up third graders tearing up his front lawn. The thought was enough to make him want to move to the city and take up accounting. Blue Thorn was taking a lot more than he was prepared to give these days.

As if she'd heard his thoughts, Gran's hand came up to cover his. "Your father would be proud of what you've done. Of what you're doing."

That struck a raw nerve. Gunner and his father hadn't seen eye to eye on anything in the years before his death. Not that Gunner had been around much to test that. He'd put Blue Thorn in his rearview mirror shortly after college, sick of Dad looking down his nose at the wild life Gunner loved. Dad's expectations had smothered Gunner, and even Gran's compassionate spirit hadn't been enough to keep him on the ranch. With his mom gone when he was seventeen, Gunner saw no point in staying where he wasn't understood. One by one his siblings had followed suit, heading off the ranch and out from underneath Gunner Senior's judgmental glare until the old man had died years later practically alone and nearly bankrupt.

Gran had written Gunner then, pleading for him to return to the ranch and save Blue Thorn. He'd come for Gran. Gunner had come to prove Dad wrong about the kind of man he was, and to overhaul Blue Thorn with his own stamp. He wasn't sure Dad would ever be proud of what he was doing here, but the sentiment raised an unwanted lump in Gunner's throat anyway.

"Click on that green arrow there," he said, not looking her in the eye. "That's how you forward an email. I'll invite them to come out, and you can stuff them full of whatever goodies you want."

He felt, rather than saw, her smile. "You'll have such fun, you wait and see."

There's where you're wrong, he thought to himself, regretting the whole thing already.

Chapter Five

Brooke scanned the rolling pastures of Blue Thorn Ranch as she drove down the road leading to Ramble Acres for another meeting Thursday. She'd never paid much attention to the landscape before in her frequent trips out to the development. Now she found herself watching the land roll by, looking for signs of the bison herd.

And, if she was honest with herself, she was watching for Gunner Buckton. After his email the other day, she had nearly picked up the phone twice to talk to him. She knew better than to judge someone by their emails, but even someone who wasn't a specialist in communications could see the man was a mix of annoyed, cornered and reluctant. But he was at least trying to be cordial—even though it seemed to physically pain him. At least it was a start. Perhaps she could really be the key to paving a useful resolution to the tensions between the Bucktons and Del-Tex. If she could foster some understanding that would make Gunner feel less under attack, as well as be a face of compassion for DelTex, then everyone would win. Including her—for Mr. Markham had gone out of his way to say that a victory here would boost her career.

They were crafting a relationship with the Bucktons, she and Audie—that much wasn't manufactured. Brooke genuinely liked the Bucktons, especially Adele. She enjoyed Audie's enthusiasm, how she'd come up with the idea for a thank-you drawing and how Audie talked to anyone who would listen about "Daisy the mama bison and how my mom got me to meet her."

The honest truth was that she owed Gunner Buckton a personal thank-you, and it was a plus for everyone if that thank-you was delivered face-to-face.

On that impulse, Brooke pulled into the ranch gate and pressed the intercom button. She wasn't meeting anyone at the Ramble Acres site—just taking photographs and picking up some preliminary floorpans—so this was an easy detour. Besides, hadn't Mr. Markham told her to use any time and resources she needed to foster the relationship? A kindly thank-you would be a wise investment of half an hour, if that.

To Brooke's surprise, Adele's voice came over the intercom.

"It's Brooke Calder, Mrs. Buckton. Audie's mom from the other day?"

"Of course I know who you are, honey. Are you at the gate?"

"I wanted to come say thanks in person, if

that's okay." Was this an imposition? Pushy? It wasn't like Brooke to second-guess herself in situations like this.

Her fears proved unfounded. "How nice of you" came Mrs. Buckton's pleased reply. "I'd love to have a visit. Do you remember how to come up to the main house?"

"Yes, ma'am."

"Okay, then. I'll buzz you in. Come on up."

Brooke felt as if she ought to ask, "Is Gunner home?"

"He's out in the pens this morning helping with vaccines. And don't worry, he doesn't bite."

Brooke indulged in a chuckle as the long metal gate rolled on its gears and drove her car down the curving lane. Today the pastures were mostly empty, but far off to her left, Brooke could see groups of bison moving about. Under a clear blue sky and among the bright green spring grass, the animals looked right out of a Western landscape painting. They drew her eye in a way cattle herds had never done—it must have been the size of them, the slow way they moved. *Majestic* seemed a grandiose word, but it was the one that came to mind. At least they looked that way from a distance. *Stubborn* had been her first impression of Daisy, and for good reason.

She drove past the barns and pens, wondering if Gunner was looking up to mutter something inhospitable as he saw her little car drive by. "I'm being nice, I'm capitalizing on a prime opportunity and I'm keeping the lines of communication open," she reminded herself as she parked on the gravel circle in front of the house's wide porch.

Adele pushed open the front door and gave a big wave. She seemed genuinely happy to see Brooke. Maybe Mrs. Buckton didn't get many visitors anymore and was glad for the company. It would be hard for such a people person as Adele Buckton to be isolated all the way out here. Brooke's public-relations side even mused that Adele might be a perfect future resident for Ramble Acres, where she'd have friends and shopping and things to do right outside her door but would still be close to the ranch.

"I'm tickled you decided to stop by!" Adele called out as she worked her way down the stairs. "I was so pleased with Audie's drawing, I had Gunner show me how to print it out, and I put it on my refrigerator."

"That's so sweet," Brooke said as she got out of the car. "Audie will love to hear that. She draws all the time."

"Well, all my grandchildren are a bit big to be playing with crayons, but I'm looking forward to the day when my great-grandchildren fill my fridge with drawings." The old woman's eyes sparkled. "Got none of those yet, but I'm a patient gal." She poked a bony elbow into Brooke's side with a wink. "I do hope some of my four grandchildren give me some great-grandbabies before the Good Lord calls me home."

"Gunner has three siblings?"

"A brother and two sisters. They're scattered all over the country right now. Gunner was the first to come on home, but I pray the others will follow in their own time."

Brooke found she liked Adele Buckton more and more. Her own mom was kind, and she'd been incredibly supportive in the first months after Jim's death, but she lacked the vibrancy Adele had. Mom always seemed tired and annoyed with the world, whereas Adele looked as if she couldn't wait to get out into it.

"You were so kind to say yes to Mrs. Cleydon's field-trip request. I was in the area, and I felt I ought to come by and say an extra thanks in person."

"Oh, well, then you ought to be thanking Gunner. He's the one who extended the invitation."

"Somehow—" Brooke leaned in "—I have a feeling he was put up to it."

Adele pulled back in mock surprise. "My, but you are as sharp as you look." She squeezed Brooke's hand. "I like to think an old gal like me still has some weight to throw around now and then."

Brooke could only laugh. "Well, I'm glad you did. Audie talks about nothing else."

Adele headed toward the door. "Oh, good. Come on in. I've got some iced tea in the fridge."

They ended up sitting on the porch for a spell—with Brooke's affection for the delightful matriarch growing every minute—before the tall figure of Gunner came out from beside the barn and stopped at the sight of the baby-blue hatchback. Brooke watched his whole posture change, as if his spine hardened right before her eyes. His steps slowed as he turned toward the house, and Brooke felt his eyes burn suspicious holes in her chest, even from a distance. He did not welcome her presence, and it showed all over Gunner's face.

Adele either didn't see—which Brooke highly doubted—or chose to ignore her grandson's annoyance, instead waving as if she had a grand surprise for Gunner. "Look who's here!" she called out.

"I can see." Gunner's voice was low and tight. "Field trip's not for another week, Ms. Calder. What brings you out our way again?"

"I had an appointment," Brooke replied, pressing on even when Gunner's eyes broadcast *I'm sure you did*, "and I wanted to say thanks to both of you. In person. For our visit and for welcoming the class. I know it's an imposition."

It sure is, Gunner's tight jaw said despite his easy, "It ain't much trouble."

"It ain't any trouble at all," Adele expanded. "Why, I have to say I love the idea of children on the ranch. We should do more of that kind of thing. Oh, that reminds me." Adele pushed herself up off the porch chair and grabbed her cane. "I have something for that darling Audie of yours. Gunner, sit yourself down and have the rest of my tea while you occupy our guest. I need to go find something in the parlor."

The minute she disappeared through the front door, Brooke put out a hand. "You don't have to stay. I'm sure you're busy."

"You're right—I am." Gunner sighed as he eased his tall body down into the porch chair. "But she'll hound me if I don't, and tea wouldn't go down so bad after twenty-four vaccinations anyhow."

He took a long drink from the glass Adele left then put it down slowly. "Don't you for one second take advantage of Gran, you hear?"

Gunner watched Brooke's eyes widen in shock. Or was it guilt?

He hadn't meant to be so abrupt, but the sight of her car on the grounds had shocked him. Gran had gone on for days about the visit with Audie, putting the girl's drawing up on the fridge, for crying out loud, latch-ing on to folks the way Gran always did. She trusted too easily. Gran believed the best in people, even when she ought to know better.

Brooke's mouth pursed as if she was swallowing the reply she really wanted to give him, and she placed her hands on the arms of the wicker chair. "I really did come here to be nice. To say thank-you for what you did for Audie and what you're going to do for the class."

He didn't believe that. "You drove all the way out here just to be nice?"

She hesitated just a moment before admitting, "Like I said, I had an appointment."

"At Ramble Acres."

"Yes. I need to take some photographs and pick up some paperwork."

"Two visits in as many weeks. Mighty convenient."

Brooke stood up and walked to the porch rail. "Mr. Buckton, I get that you're no fan of DelTex."

No fan was an understatement, but he let that slide.

"And I understand that you care about your family's property. But I'm not your enemy. I'm not out to hoodwink you or your grandmother. I'd like to help you find a solution to a difficult situation." She turned to look at him, leaning up against the rail. "Have you ever thought that maybe neither party really understands the other here? That instead of locking horns with DelTex, you could talk to each other and find a solution that's better for everybody?"

Gunner stood up. "Well, don't you sound like a glossy brochure."

She crossed her arms over her chest. "I write those glossy brochures." Her chin jutted up in a defiant gesture that almost made him laugh. "It's my job to help DelTex communicate with their customers and the community."

Gunner sat back on one hip. "You mean help them look the other way while DelTex steals honest people's land?"

She took a step toward him. She had

fight in her, and that intrigued him. "That's not fair."

"Oh, there's a lot about this that's not fair."

"Mercy, Gunner, can't I leave you alone for ten seconds without you picking a fight?" Gran practically skewered him in the ribs with her cane as she came out the door.

"It's all right," Brooke said, smoothing her curls back from the breeze and slanting a dark look at Gunner. "It's not as if I didn't expect this."

"Well, you shouldn't need to expect this. Not when you're a guest on the Blue Thorn." Gunner noticed what Gran was carrying and rolled his eyes as she placed a small stuffed bison into Brooke Calder's hand. "This is for Audie. My granddaughter Ellie knits them for us to give out to visitors as a souvenir." She looked right at Gunner. "Only, we don't get so many visitors lately."

"Gran..."

"Don't you *Gran* me, young man."

Brooke had the sweet surprised look down

to an art form. "That's very kind of you, Mrs. Buckton, but I…"

"Call me Adele, won't you?" Gran sidled over next to Brooke as if they were old friends.

That was the last straw. Gunner took off his hat and glared at Gran. "You know who she works for. Can't you see why she's here?"

Gran pulled herself up and stared at Gunner, even though she had to crane her neck back to look him in the eye. "She works for that company we don't like, and she's here being nice and saying thank-you for a kindness. She's being a mature adult in a less than perfect situation, which you don't seem to be able to do. Have I gotten all the details right?"

Gunner wanted to stomp off the porch and have no part of this business, but Gran would never stand for it. When Gran got like this, she was liable to grab him by the ear and yank him back onto the porch if he tried to get away. Instead, he merely stuffed his hands into his pockets and said nothing.

Gran turned back to Brooke. "You folks at DelTex want the land by the northwest creek, am I right?"

"I believe so," Brooke replied.

"You know so." Gunner tried not to grind the answer out through his teeth.

"Have you seen the land by the creek, Brooke?"

"No." Brooke's eyes showed she could see where this was heading exactly like he could.

"Well, then, I would *like*," Gran said, giving the word an emphasis that declared it a demand rather than a suggestion, "for you to take Brooke out there and show her what all the fuss is about. Have a conversation instead of a standoff." She looked at Brooke. "I take it you can spare the time?"

Brooke at least looked smart enough to know she had *better* spare the time when Gran put it that way. "I'd much rather have a conversation than a standoff. I'd be happy to take a look at the creek."

Gunner swallowed the irritating sensation of being a twelve-year-old boy who'd been told to mind his chores. He was now legally the head of Blue Thorn Ranch, but no one on the property ever dared to defy Gran, and now surely wasn't the time for him to try. "Well, fine, then. We'll *converse*. We'll take my truck." He looked down to check that she had sensible shoes on for such a trip. "At least you're not in high heels or anything."

Brooke's chin jutted out. "As a matter of fact, I've got a pair of boots in my trunk for when I take Audie to riding lessons." Her eyes practically shouted "So there!"

As she walked off to the little blue car, Gunner pondered what he could safely say to Gran for her little stunt.

She beat him to the punch. "I know exactly what you're thinking, so don't start. I like her, but I'm no fool. I think she's genuinely being nice, but I get that she may have motives like you suspect. So calm yourself down, be nice to her and think of it this way—it often pays to keep your enemies close."

Gunner raised an eyebrow at this cunning side of his grandmother.

She pointed up at him. "But it pays far better to not have enemies at all. And that comes from talking and listening. Something you'd better learn to do a bit more of if you're gonna make it in life, son. No one wins a standoff—most times there are only two losers."

He bit back the urge to argue further. After all, he could spend the next half hour showing a pretty lady one of his favorite parts of Blue Thorn Ranch, or he could spend it forcing large hairy beasts into a small pen so he could stab them with a big needle. Some decisions were easier than others.

Pulling the keys from his pocket, he gave Gran an "I can play nice" smile and hit the remote ignition. The dark blue pickup roared to life.

Brooke walked back in a pair of tooled cowboy boots that changed the look of her outfit completely. This was definitely a better choice than vaccines. After all, both might hurt for a bit, but maybe like the shots, this might do him well in the long run.

He opened the door for her. "Hop in," he said, tipping his hat and offering his hand to help her climb into the high cab.

She slid right past his outstretched hand. "Thanks, I will." And with an ease he knew she meant for him to see, she nimbly stepped up and settled herself in the passenger seat.

As he pulled the truck around to head out toward the creek, he turned to Brooke. "Wave at Gran like this will be loads of fun." He gave an exaggerated wave to match the old woman's wide grin from the porch.

Brooke complied. "Won't it?"

Gunner looked right at his passenger. "That depends on you."

Chapter Six

Brooke stood on the low ridge and took in the spectacular view. The strong sun warmed the early-spring breeze to keep the weather pleasant. There was something awe-inspiring about huge stretches of Texan pastures, especially as the bluebonnets began to fill the land. She loved Austin, loved her little house in her colorful neighborhood on the edge of that city, but a place like this somehow sank under the skin and fed the soul. It wasn't hard to see why men—and women like Adele—fought so hard to keep land like this.

Gunner pointed down to a copse of trees on the far side of the creek. "There was a time you could fish right there. I'd spend hours with Luke seeing who could catch the biggest fish."

"And who won?" She shaded her eyes with her hand as she looked where he pointed.

"I did, of course."

The clear pride in his voice drew her eyes back to Gunner. "And just for the record, how big was this prize-winning fish?"

He grinned, caught in his boasting as she knew he was. "A staggering eight inches."

She laughed. "Oh. A whopper of a fish, then."

"Beat Luke's seven-incher, and that's all that counted." He began walking a little farther down the ridge. "This isn't just real estate or a drainage system, Ms. Calder. Not to me."

"Brooke," she corrected before she could even think about it. Ms. Calder was her professional self, and this was feeling more and more personal. Anyway, the more each side could see each other as people rather than obstacles, the better off everyone would be.

And it wasn't hard to look at Gunner as a man rather than a professional goal. Tall with sandy-blond hair and those extraordinary turquoise Buckton eyes, he was no slouch to look at for any reason. There was more to him than handsome features, however. The part of her that felt unmoored since Jim's death was drawn to the grounded way Gunner talked about his land.

"Okay, Brooke, I just want to be clear here. I'm not interested in selling off one inch of Blue Thorn. Ever. So as long as you're square with that, I'm willing to play it friendly." He reached down and plucked a stem of grass. "I guard what's mine. It may have taken me a while to find my way back to the Blue Thorn, but make no mistake—I'm here for good, and I'm not letting any of it go."

She nodded, feeling such a show of loyalty deserved her respect, even if it did pose a growing challenge. "I get that." She sat down on the trunk of a large, fallen-over tree that sat under the shadow of its neighbor—a great, sprawling live oak that threw a pleasant patch of shade over the lovely spot. Insects buzzed around her, mingling with the cry of a pair of hawks. "I'm not some heartless corporate shark, you know."

Gunner surprised her by sitting down a few feet away, still twirling the blade of grass between his fingers. "No, you just work for one."

"I could give you a whole speech about how DelTex has done some great things for the region, but somehow I think it would fall on deaf ears. You don't strike me as the kind of man who changes his mind often."

He laughed at that. "No, ma'am. I prefer to call it single-minded. Gran has a few other names for it."

Now she laughed. "I can imagine." She sat back, breathing in the wonderful scents of the land. "She's amazing, your grandmother.

The whole place is beautiful. If you don't mind my asking, what made you stay away so long?"

Gunner shook his head with a sound that was too dark to be called a laugh. "So now I know you didn't grow up here. I hardly ever run into folks who don't know my... colorful...history."

"Jim, my late husband—" it still amazed her that she could say that without it gripping her throat anymore "—he's the one who grew up here. I grew up down by Galveston. He might have known you."

Gunner looked at her. "Wait—your husband was Jimmy Calder, wasn't he?"

"So you did know him?"

"I knew of him. He graduated from high school a few years ahead of me. We didn't exactly run in the same crowd."

She could imagine, but she asked anyway, wanting to hear his version of it. "How's that?"

Gunner leaned back on his elbows, crossing his boots as his long legs stretched out in front of him. Boots, hat, jeans, lanky ease—he looked every inch the Texas cowboy. "Well, let's just say that while your man was leading Bible studies in the school cafeteria, I was most likely sneaking cigarettes and kisses out behind it. I knew who he was, but I expect he only knew me as one of the lost souls he'd failed to reach."

That was Jim. If men could be born missionaries, Jim was. His faith was total, fiery and enthralling from the moment she'd met him. The vision of him leading studies in college, brown eyes lit with purpose and enthusiasm, bloomed up out of her memory. They'd married while still in school. She was glad she could think of him now without falling apart. He'd never have wanted her to mourn his loss for long, but the knowledge of his joy in heaven hadn't ever made the torment of being left behind any easier to bear.

Gunner's voice, far gentler than she'd ever heard it before, brought her out of her thoughts. "I'm sorry for your loss. And Audie's. What happened to him?"

Brooke pulled in a deep breath. She was almost at the point where she could feel the story honored him and his faith instead of just breaking her heart—almost. "We were in Africa—Chad, to be exact—in the mission field. One of the local government officials had been commandeering goods and funds meant for the school we served. Jim could never stand that sort of thing."

She sent her eyes out across the slow current of water, not quite able to look at Gunner as she told the rest of the story. "He tried all kinds of ways to stop the corruption, but nothing ever worked. One night some medicine meant for one of our students was waylaid and found its way to the black market. That was the last straw for him. He went down to this man and accused him of theft in front of the village elders. No one from the village was willing to cross this goon's path, but Jim was." She swallowed hard. "He never came home."

"That's awful. I'm sorry."

"They found him just before dawn. Shot in the back, they told me. Not quite an execution, but close enough. Audie was six. We gathered our things, came home to Texas and Friday Taco Trio became Friday Tacos for Two."

She was glad Gunner didn't feel the need to spout any of the sympathy-card phrases that story usually produced. The quiet and the open space seemed to hold the moment in a respect that didn't need words. After a long pause, Brooke sighed and said, "Hey, wait a minute, you were supposed to be telling me about *your* colorful history."

Gunner angled toward her. "Nothing much to tell. If there was a way to be wild, mouth off, get in trouble or mess up, I did it. I was never quite arrested, but I came close a number of times. I kept my daddy up nights, and Gran will tell you there are dents in my bed from where she rested her elbows on it praying I'd come home in one piece."

She'd said her share of "bring him home safe, Lord" prayers over Jim—if for entirely different reasons—and she knew the ache of those night vigils. "And your mama?"

"She passed when I was a teenager. She was sick for a spell before she died, and my dad didn't handle that well. He wanted me to take care of my siblings on account of how young they were—Ellie was thirteen and the twins, Luke and Tess, were only eleven—only, I wasn't interested in doin' as I was told. No, I lashed out in all the ways teenagers do—and then some. Soon as I could manage it, I left."

"Where did you go? When you left the Blue Thorn, I mean."

"Oh, anywhere that was away. Did a stint at college, but that didn't last long. I bummed around Texas for a while, working ranches and the like, but then that didn't feel far enough. Four years later, I ended up working on a boat in Oregon."

"Wow." Brooke laughed. "You really did run far and long."

"Actually, I was considering some oil-field work in Alaska when Gran wrote me to say Dad was sick and asked me to come back."

"What made you say yes?"

Gunner thought for a moment before replying. "I didn't, at first. Then Dad got sicker and Gran asked again. I knew she would never ask twice if things weren't desperate. Only I didn't hurry. By the time I wandered on home, the herd was all but gone and Dad had passed on. I suppose some part of me figured it was time to come back and see if staying put was any better than running."

Brooke watched a butterfly float by and land. It waved its yellow wings back and forth before lifting off again, this time settling on the far end of the log. "And was it?"

Pushing his hat farther down on his head, Gunner looked out over the land. "I'm still working on that, but yeah, it seems to be. I feel like I've made my dent in the world, starting up a healthy herd like this. Cattle were never really my thing, but the idea of raising bison, of keeping the species viable and all when a century ago they were just about done for? That feeds something. If that doesn't sound too hokey to say."

It didn't sound hokey at all. Brooke had always admired men who stood for something. Until now, she'd just seen Gunner Buckton as a man who stood against DelTex. Sitting here listening to him gave her a glimpse of why he acted the way he did. Understanding was the foundation for communication. "Thank you for bringing me here."

There was a bit of amazement in his eyes—a surprise she felt tumble her own stomach—before he said, "You're welcome."

If this afternoon was any indication, it wouldn't be so hard to build a relationship with the Bucktons, to keep the conversation going. In fact, it might be downright nice.

* * *

"Glad that's over." Billy came in from the holding pens looking hot and tired. Containing huge adult bison was a tricky, even dangerous business. No one confined a one-thousand-pound beast and expected it to cooperate for vaccines—even with a series of ever-narrowing feeder chutes and tight metal holding pens, the whole process felt like trying to herd a mountain range.

Gunner checked the chart Billy handed him. "Everyone looking okay?"

"Herd's healthy. Looks like we'll have a strong spring calving season." Billy smiled—that was good news. Several of the bison bellowed on their way out to pasture, registering their displeasure at the checkup.

"Roscoe's getting to be quite the handful, but I think we'll be fine once mating season is done in August."

"Those bulls can get ornery," Gunner commiserated.

"You oughta know," Billy teased. He nodded toward the blue car now heading down the lane toward the exit. "How'd it go?"

Gunner looked after the car as it raised a cloud of dust in its wake. "I'm not sure."

"What do you mean by that?"

"I'm pretty sure she's up to something. I'm just not sure what it is."

Billy took a bandanna out of his pocket and wiped his forehead. "You said she works for DelTex. Shouldn't be too hard to guess."

"Yeah, well, if it was Markham, I'd say it'd be easy. He'd be here trying to get us to sell."

"If it was Markham, you wouldn't let him in the gate."

Gunner began walking toward the supply room. "That's just it. They could be sending her because they know I won't talk to Markham. Only, she talks like she's brokering some kind of treaty, as if she expects to find some solution that makes everybody happy."

Billy kicked a stone out of his way. "Ain't no such thing. Not in this case."

"That's just it—there isn't a solution like that here." Gunner took the clipboard Billy had given him and hung it on a nail in the wall. "Either they get the land or we keep the land. Why is she here looking for a compromise when there isn't one?"

Billy stuffed his gloves in the pocket of his jeans. "Maybe she just wants to gaze at your ugly mug. And you hers. She's definitely your type. Think they know that?"

Gunner whacked his hat across Billy's chest. "Would DelTex stoop that low? Try to lower my defenses with a pair of pretty legs?"

"It's been known to work on you before," Billy said.

"Not anymore, it doesn't."

"You say that, but who invited a bunch of third graders to come eat brownies and ice cream on the lawn?"

Gunner didn't care to answer that. He just walked out of the barn to leave Billy whistling.

Chapter Seven

Gunner was starting to think maybe Billy had a point. He watched the little blue car make its way up the drive Saturday morning and wondered if his defenses really had come down. He'd told Billy there was no way a woman could send his wits packing, but based on the phone call he'd made this morning, he'd have to eat those words.

He told himself not to smile as Audie tumbled out of the car, heading toward him at a full-out run. The little girl slammed into him like a pint-size wall of happiness, nearly knocking him over as she hugged him around the waist.

"I'm so glad. I'm so, so, *so* glad you called and are gonna let me see the calf!" she said with her head still buried in his stomach. Daisy had given birth Thursday night, and all he could think about since was how much Audie would get a kick out of seeing the brand-new baby bison.

"Whoa there, girl. It's not that big a deal." He caught Brooke's eyes over Audie's head, and the expression in them told Gunner just how big a deal it was to the Calder women. The people-pleasing stuff was supposed to be Gran's stock and trade, not his.

"It is, Mr. Buckton. It's a *huge* deal." Audie looked up at him with big brown eyes and a smile that went from ear to ear. Looking at him like that, she could have asked him for just about anything, and Gunner couldn't hope to refuse. She was too cute for her own good, Audie was.

She took after her mother that way.

Brooke had reached Gunner by now, all smiles herself. She held her hands together as if she didn't know what else to do with them, and Gunner had the unsettling thought that she was trying to keep herself from hugging him. For a split second, with Audie's arms locked around his middle, he wondered what it would feel like to have Brooke's arms around him. *Stop right there*, he told himself. *The innocent little kid is one thing, but this mama's got designs. Don't you forget that.*

"Thanks for this," Brooke said, looking as if she really did mean it. "You didn't have to."

"It's self-defense, actually," Gunner admitted—and it was true, sort of. "I knew Audie'd want to see the calf when Daisy delivered, and it wouldn't be smart to have the whole class over there when they come next week."

"You're right, you're right," Audie said, pulling back to start tugging Gunner's sleeve toward the pen. "I'd just *die* if I knew Daisy's baby had been born and I couldn't see." Gunner had to stop himself from laughing at Audie's dramatic overture. He couldn't bring himself to dampen her enthusiasm— he was still a bit in awe himself about every new bison born on Blue Thorn land. For a species that had come so close to extinction, every new calf was a tiny victory, a small payback for all the wrong mankind had done to the animal.

He hunched down to Audie's height, looking her straight in the eye. "I'm glad to know you're so excited. And I'm glad I can show you the little fella, but—"

"Fella!" Audie cried, jumping up in glee. "So Daisy did get a baby boy calf!"

"She did, indeed." Gunner laughed even as he took Audie by both shoulders. "But brand-new mamas need to be handled with extra care. You're gonna have to get all your squiggles and squealing out of your system before we go anywhere near the corral.

Daisy and her calf need quiet. And we can't get too close."

"You mean I can't touch him?" Gunner couldn't believe how the disappointment in Audie's eyes poked him right in the gut. "You said the new calves are so soft."

"They are. And I'll try and make sure you get the chance to pet him someday. It just can't be today. He needs to imprint on his mama and no one else. Not even me."

"Imprint?" Audie's nose crinkled up in confusion.

Gunner looked up at Brooke, at a bit of a loss for how to explain familial bonding to an eight-year-old.

Brooke came down to Audie's level so that the three of them made a short little trio right there on the house lawn. "Mama-baby love. Like you and I when you were a baby. You knew who I was just as strong as I knew who you were. Only some animals—like bison— need to do it all alone and right away."

That wasn't entirely accurate—bonding

happened in the midst of a herd—but it was a good enough explanation for Audie. "It's so the little guy can always find Daisy and knows it's Daisy who'll take care of him. If he bonded to you or me, then he'd always be looking to us to take care of him."

Audie's chin jutted out. "I'd do it."

Gunner watched himself reach out and ruffle Audie's brown waves as if the hand belonged to some other man. *I don't like kids. Why do I like this one so much?* "I bet you would." Then, as if again some other nice guy had taken over, Gunner found himself saying, "That's why I'm gonna let you name him."

Brooke and Audie's mutual joyful shock did something warm and wiggly to Gunner's stomach. Billy was right. He was in trouble here.

"Really?" Audie's eyes were as big as a cow's, the word squealed out of her with a full-blown glee no adult could ever hope to match.

"Gunner." Brooke's tone was soft and astonished. "You don't have to do that."

He hadn't planned to offer Audie the right to name the calf. Usually, he kept that honor for himself, Billy or Gran. There was just something about Audie that pulled all this nice out of him—nice he didn't even know he had. "It's mine to give. I've been running out of good names lately anyhow." He looked down at Audie, who had only just now stopped jumping up and down. "You strike me as someone good at naming."

The bit of tears he saw hanging on Brooke's lashes gave him a jolt. She kept surprising him, kept knocking down whatever he thought he knew about her.

"Oh, I am. I'm *splendid* at names." Audie drew the word out as if it was a favorite.

"Okay, then. Looks like we've got the right person for the job." Gunner stood up and began walking toward the corral. "The first thing you need to know about bison calves is that they're orange."

It had just the effect he thought it would. Audie stopped in her tracks, amazement rounding her mouth to the cutest little "oh" shape, eyes wide.

"Yep. They're not brown like the big bison. They're a rusty-orange color. Gran says they're cute and cuddly, but they aren't. They're wild animals, and their mamas can be as fierce as your mama."

"Oh, I know," Audie said, taking the bait. "And you haven't even seen my mama when she's mad."

Gunner allowed himself the luxury of a long look at Brooke as they began walking again. "No, Miss Audie, I have not. Except, of course, when she gave Miss Daisy a few dark looks about blocking the road the other day."

Brooke's eyes took on a glint Gunner felt in the pit of his stomach. "I was as polite as can be to that bison."

He chose not to hide the smile that crept up from that part of his stomach. "I never said you weren't. But I've known plenty of women who could have fine manners and be fierce as coyotes at the same time." They approached the far corral fence. "Remember what I said now—keep quiet, stay your distance, you do what I say."

"Yes, sir, Mr. Buckton."

Brooke couldn't quite work out where this side of Gunner Buckton came from. The kind man before her, the one who talked to Audie as if she was the smartest girl he'd ever known, as if her relentless curiosity was a gift instead of the trial it often was—this Gunner Buckton couldn't be the same man who'd stubbornly dug his heels in and stopped his ears to any offers DelTex had made. The look in his eye as he caught her gaze just before they reached the fence made her breath hitch and her stomach do a flip it hadn't done in years. And Audie's face? Well, if that man blocked every single thing she and DelTex did from here on in, she'd still owe him one for her daughter's joy today.

The far corral where he'd put Daisy to calve was cool and quiet, shaded by a big oak and away from the rest of the herd. At the far end stood Daisy and a calf.

The young bison looked to be the size of a collie, coming maybe to Audie's waist, and bore a rusty-orange color just as Gunner had described. *Cute* probably wasn't the right word, but the beast was fuzzy and friendly looking, new and cautious standing right up next to his mama.

Gunner, Audie and Brooke crouched down along the fence. Daisy swung her head toward Gunner, and Brooke would have sworn she saw a mother's protective vigilance in the bison's big brown eyes.

Audie cupped a hand to Gunner's ear as if they'd known each other for years and whispered, "He can walk already?"

"Stood up not half an hour after he was born and was running around that afternoon," Gunner said. "Of course, he's already shown he's not the type to wait around. Most of the other bison won't calve for a few weeks yet. Seems our little guy was impatient to get out into the world."

"But he's okay?" Brooke's friend had given birth to a precariously premature baby a month ago, and Audie clearly remembered those touch-and-go first days.

Gunner's smile was reassuring. "Fit as a fiddle, near as I can tell." He caught Brooke's eyes over Audie's head again. "Billy says everything is fine, and Daisy isn't worried one bit. I'd say the little guy must know it's a big deal to be the first calf of the year."

"He's smart," Audie proclaimed. "He looks it. He wanted to be first."

"That's what Billy says." He peered down at Audie. "Do the bison talk to you, too?"

That sent Audie into a torrent of hushed giggles that she tried to hide behind her hands. "No, silly. I'm just guessing."

They sat in silence for a few minutes,

watching the mama bison and her calf. Brooke found her gaze continually wandering to Gunner, an odd mix of puzzlement and wonder tumbling around her chest. This wasn't the man she'd met in the road only a few days ago. This wasn't the man Mr. Markham was prepared to battle for a slice of land. And then again, Gunner Buckton was that man, too, wasn't he? There was a dark, lonesome edge to his features that spoke of the time he'd spent trying to put the ranch permanently in his past. If ever a man could look like a conflict, this man did.

And yet Gunner looked perfectly at home on the Blue Thorn; born to it, bred to lead it, serious about his new role. Aware, it seemed, that not everyone was confident about his ability to handle this position. The people at DelTex treated him as Adele's chosen heir, but not as his own man. Mr. Markham had encouraged her to craft a relationship with Adele rather than try to convince Gunner. Clearly, Mr. Markham thought Gunner immovable, but he didn't seem to view that as an impossible obstacle since he believed that Adele still wielded control.

When Gunner somehow sensed her gaze and turned to look at her, Brooke felt her cheeks redden at being caught staring. For a moment his eyes took on a bad-boy mischievous gleam, an "I caught you" superiority, but then it softened into a quiet curiosity. A questioning glance that told Brooke Gunner was having just as much trouble figuring out who she was.

In that moment, it became all too clear that they were two people who weren't supposed to like each other, stuck trying to work out what to do about the fact that they *did* like each other.

With an eight-year-old thrown in for extra confusion. *Complicated* didn't even begin to cover it.

"We probably should go now," Gunner said quietly.

"I think you're right," Audie agreed in a

very grown-up voice. "Oh, wait, wait," she cried in a whisper as the baby calf took a few steps. "He's moving."

The little orange calf began walking, as did Daisy. Gunner, Audie and Brooke were already standing, but stopped moving. Daisy gave a low moan, a commanding snort and then headed right toward them with the calf at her side.

"Well, look at that," Gunner said softly. "Nobody move."

Audie gave a little gasp as Daisy and her calf crossed the small pen to stand so close Brooke could have reached out and touched the beast's enormous black nose. It felt as if Daisy was staring right at her—a hushed, wondrous moment that both frightened and fascinated her. The calf was eye to eye with Audie. Mama to mama and child to child— Brooke knew no one would believe her if that was how she described this surreal moment, but the connection was undeniable.

"Mama," Audie said quietly, her voice filled with awe.

"I see it, baby. I feel it," Brooke whispered.

With a final great burst of breath, Daisy and her calf turned and began walking toward the other side of the pen.

Brooke let out the breath she'd been holding. Audie whispered a muted squeal. Gunner put one foot on the pen fence and shook his head. "I don't know what all that was, but I have never, ever seen anything like that happen before." His voice reflected the amazing sensation that currently ran down Brooke's spine. "She came right up to you."

"I think she was telling me to make sure I think up a really good name," Audie said.

"You think? Well, who am I to argue with that?" Gunner said, catching Brooke's eye again. "Now I'm extra sure we have the right person for the job."

"I'm gonna have to think long and hard," Audie said, her eyebrows scrunched up as if she was already deep into the task. "This is important."

As they walked back toward the house, Adele came onto the porch. Audie ran up to the woman as if they'd known each other for years. "Guess what, Mrs. Buckton? Guess what happened?"

Brooke held back, half to let Audie describe the encounter to Adele on her own and half to talk to Gunner. "You want to tell me what just happened over there?" she asked.

He looked at her as he ran his hand across his chin. "I was hoping you could tell me."

"I thought you said new mothers didn't like human interaction when they calved."

Gunner adjusted his hat as he looked over toward Audie and Adele. "That's just it. They don't. I've got no more explanation for what we just saw than you do." He stared at Brooke as if she were a puzzle to be solved. "She looked right at you. I mean *right at* you."

"I know," Brooke said. Something important had just happened, but she couldn't say what. Or why. "Does that happen to you, when she looks at you like that?"

"That sort of sink-right-through-you feeling? Like she knows something you never told anyone?"

It felt reassuring to have someone else put it into words. She wasn't going crazy—at least not yet. "Yes. Gunner, this is too weird for me."

"What? You don't want to be a bison whisperer?"

Brooke stepped away. "That's insane. There's a rational explanation for what just happened over there, and I want you to give it to me."

Gunner sat down on one of the lawn's picnic benches. "Most animals have a natural trust instinct, even wild ones. They'll decide—sometimes quickly, more often over a long time—that certain humans can be trusted. You know when they say someone has a way with animals? That's usually what it means. I'd say you just got a whopping dose under highly unusual circumstances."

Brooke sat down on the same bench. "So Daisy's up and decided she likes me? After that standoff in the road earlier?"

Gunner laughed. "I suppose you could say that. Could be that Daisy senses how much Audie likes her and the little guy. Animals can sense fear, so I reckon they can sense affection, too. You and Audie told her she could trust you with her calf." Taking off his hat and running his hand through his hair, he added, "That's the only explanation I got. I mean, Audie did it to me, too. I can't tell you why I up and called you to come and see the calf. I just did. Mostly 'cause I knew how much Audie would like it. And…" He shook his head and didn't finish the sentence.

Brooke knew why.

Chapter Eight

Audie's head bowed over her bedspread. "God bless Mama, and Daddy in heaven, and Nana and Grandpa in Oklahoma, and Hammie. Help Maria get over her strip throat, and Pastor Summers with his broken leg."

Her daughter's bedtime prayers were often the highlight of Brooke's day. Audie had such a tender heart, praying for everything from a friend's "strip throat" to the class hamster to the pastor's recent riding accident. Brooke could kneel beside her daughter and feel as if God had blessed her no matter how trying the day had been.

"Take care of Daisy and her calf. Keep 'em safe and healthy and thank You for me getting to see them today. Thank You for Mr. Buckton and Grannie Buckton and how nice they are to us. And help me come up with an extra-special name for the baby bison. Amen."

"Amen," Brooke agreed, smiling as she ran a hand through Audie's fresh-out-of-the-bath curls. "You pray the best prayers, baby."

Audie hopped up into the bed and burrowed under the sheets. Right next to her on the pillow was the stuffed bison from Blue Thorn Ranch. "Grannie Buckton?" Brooke inquired as she tucked the linens in place around her daughter.

Audie grinned. "That's what Mrs. Buckton said I should call her. She says all her special friends call her Grannie."

"It's nice to have special friends. Especially ones as nice as—" Brooke tried out the name, wondering if she needed permission to use it "—Grannie Buckton. That was a really nice thing she and Mr. Buckton did for you today."

"He's really nice. He wasn't at first, but he sure is now. I didn't think he smiled much when I first met him, but you seem to make him smile more."

Brooke wasn't quite sure what to say to that. "Sometimes people change when you get to know them." It seemed safer to find a new topic of conversation than her changing opinion of Gunner Buckton. "Have you thought of a name yet?"

"Well, just Rusty, so far." Audie yawned. "But I don't think that's special enough."

"He does need a special name, I agree. You keep thinking on it, and I'm sure you'll come up with just the right one. After all, Daisy's given you the job as much as Mr. Buckton did."

Audie's eyes lit up at the memory of that time by the pen. "She did, didn't she?"

"I sure think so." Anything that made Audie feel special was a fine thing to

Brooke's thinking. She watched that wondrous moment when Audie began to close her eyes and nod off. Audie was such a gift, such an amazing little girl and so very much like her father.

"Can we look it up in your 'like word' book after church tomorrow?" Audie asked through heavily lidded eyes.

"Look up what, baby?"

"Rusty. I need a special word for that rusty color."

Brooke laughed softly. "Sure thing. We'll get my thesaurus out over lunch and look up any word you like."

Duly satisfied, Audie snuggled farther into her blankets, tucked the stuffed bison under her chin and drifted off. *She's such a gift, Lord—thank You for giving her to me*, Brooke prayed as she settled the blankets and switched off the light. The cut tin night-light Jim had brought back from one of his trips filled the room with tiny glowing stars. "So that you dream of heaven," he'd told Audie as a baby the night he plugged it in for the first time. *She's my shining star, my light in the dark. I don't know what I'd do without her. I see Jim every time I look at her. Thank You that it doesn't hurt so much anymore.*

All today was a gift, Brooke thought as she moved through the quiet house. The work week had been hectic, but today at Blue Thorn had been nothing short of amazing. Each time she drove out through those ranch gates, she found herself wondering when she could return. The affection she was coming to feel for the Bucktons and Blue Thorn Ranch would help her in keeping the conversation open with DelTex. She was coming to a valuable place where she could relate to both sides, and that was good for communication, good for a solution.

But it's more than that. It's becoming personal. Very personal. And I'm not sure what to do about that.

Putting a load of laundry in, Brooke dialed her mother's number. "Hi, Gary, is Mom around?" she asked when her stepfather answered the phone.

"Just putting away the ice cream," Gary said, and Brooke could hear the smile in his voice. Dessert after dinner was a family tradition—one that still threatened her waistline to this day.

"Hi, sweetheart" came her mother's voice. "It's nice to hear from you. Everything okay?"

Brooke pretreated a nasty grape-jelly stain on one of Audie's favorite shirts as she held the phone to her ear with one shoulder. "Everything's fine. Audie and I had a bit of an adventure today. I wanted to tell you about it."

"Oh, well, let me get my bowl of fudge brickle and I'll be all ears."

Brooke related the story of the visit and the calf, careful not to sound too surreal about the wondrous connection with the animals. "You should have seen Audie's face when Gunner told her she could name the calf, Mom. I thought she was going to explode."

"Oh, I can just imagine. What fun for her!"

"Mom…" Brooke stood still, wanting to get the words right. "Gunner's mother asked Audie to call her Grannie Buckton. I wasn't sure you'd be okay with that."

"Oh, sweetheart, you're kind to ask, but of course I'm okay with that. A girl can't have too many grannies in this world if you ask me."

"She calls you Nana, and she's never known Jim's mother, but still I wanted to ask."

After a bit of a pause, Brooke's mother softened her tone. "Why do I get the feeling that's not the real reason you called? Are you sure you're okay?"

Mom's intuition when it came to her had always been dead-on. "Well, I suppose you're right. Only I don't know how to ask what I want to ask. What I think I want to ask, that is. I'm not even sure I should be asking in the first place."

Mom chuckled softly. "Why don't you try just asking?"

Brooke closed her eyes and took a deep breath. "When did you know?"

"When did I know what?"

Dive in, just dive in. "When you met Gary. When did you know you had healed enough from Dad's passing?"

"Oh, my. That is a big question." Mom thought a moment, and Brooke could hear the spoon scrape against the ice-cream bowl. "I suppose it was when I met Gary, and I didn't find myself comparing every little thing about him to your father. When I could see him as his own man, not just someone who wasn't Bill."

Brooke tried to think of a reply, but couldn't. This felt like such strange, new, scary territory.

"It's been two years, Brooke. You're so much younger than I was. You deserve a chance to start again."

Brooke's throat turned dry while her eyes

welled up. "I'm not sure." Some days Oklahoma seemed so far away—why hadn't she moved back there when Jim died?

"You haven't even been on a date since you lost Jim. Discovering you're interested in someone doesn't mean everything has to change right now."

"It feels so big. Too big. I'm not sure I'm ready. And the situation—well, it's less than ideal." Brooke sank down onto the laundry room floor, her back up against the humming dryer. "It's a complicated work thing. I feel like I can't do complicated. Especially with Audie."

"Does Audie like this Gunner fellow? It is this Gunner fellow we're talking about, isn't it?"

It felt dangerous to say it out loud. "Yes, it's Gunner. And I think she likes him now. He was rather awful when we first met." She'd already told her mother the whole story of Daisy and the standoff in the road. "But he's been so different lately."

"Well, that certainly sounds promising. Has he asked you out? Shown any of that kind of interest?"

If only it was that simple. "Not exactly. But because of work and this bison thing we've spent some time together. And, well, something's there, you know? I'm thinking about possibilities for the first time. It's scary."

"Of course it is. But Jim would never have wanted you to be alone, and he would want a father for Audie. I'm not saying it has to be this man, but if you think there could be something between you and it might be good for Audie, don't let fear keep you from trying."

Brooke swiped a tear from her cheek with one of Audie's T-shirts. "Is it time?"

"Only you know that, sunshine. But if you're asking me if it *could* be time? I'd say your heart will tell you. Take a small step forward and see what happens. I'll say a prayer that your heart tells you to stop if you're not ready. But know this—you'll never be totally ready."

"Yeah, I know." Brooke felt small and fragile, wanting to clutch at Audie's pajamas like a teddy bear and crawl into her mother's lap.

"I'll tell you one thing, though." Brooke could hear a tear or two in her mother's voice. "I sure am glad God sent Gary into my life. And I don't love your father one bit less for loving Gary. Do you?"

Gary had been an amazing stepfather. He'd never tried to replace her dad, but he'd stood in the gap Dad had left with such grace and strength. Audie had never known Brooke's father, and Gary had been wonderful to his step-granddaughter. Mom always said love was elastic, stretching to fill any place where it was needed.

"No, Mom. Gary's great. For you, for me and for Audie." She sniffed a little. "And you tell him that for me."

"Hearts can love more than once, Brooke.

They have to heal first, but they can love many, many times."

Brooke called Jim's face up from memory, heard his voice and remembered the way he used to kiss the back of her neck. There was loss and memory, but the pain wasn't sharp and crippling anymore. There was a space in her heart now. A healed but empty place. Maybe it *was* time.

Gunner leaned back on the truck fender and watched Daisy with her calf. He'd been here since after Sunday supper, and it was getting on near 11:00 p.m.—his days started early on the ranch, and he'd feel it in the morning if he didn't drag himself away and get to bed.

Still, he couldn't seem to make himself go. Since yesterday's visit with Brooke and Audie, the orange calf consumed his thoughts. The little guy seemed perfectly healthy despite his early arrival—in no need of special care—and yet Gunner found himself totally preoccupied with him and Daisy.

Okay, that wasn't exactly true. What really preoccupied him was what had happened with Daisy and the calf when he brought Brooke and Audie out to the pen. That sort of spiritual animal-connection thing was Billy's territory, not his. He loved his work, and was passionate about conserving the species, but this wasn't any of those things. This was something else, something he couldn't explain. Probably shouldn't explain, given that just about anyone would think him crazy if he tried.

He'd switched his cell phone to vibrate in order to keep things quiet for the calf and mama, so Gunner kept his voice low as he answered the call that came buzzing in his back pocket.

"Hey, Els, how's Hotlanta?"

"Cookin' fine, big brother." Gunner's little sister Ellie was enjoying a snazzy career in promotions for a chain of restaurants in Atlanta. Her job probably had a lot in common with Brooke's, now that he thought about it. Their personal lives couldn't be more different, though. Ellie was single, successful and just starting a serious relationship with one of the city's rising star chefs. "We're in negotiations to land Derek a regular spot on the morning news."

"Tomorrow's Food Network star?" Gunner laughed, and Daisy looked up at him as if to shush her owner. "I gotta talk quiet—I'm by the pen with the new calf."

"Gran said Daisy calved early. Everything okay?"

"It is, but the little guy's fine."

"What did you name him?"

Gunner found himself hesitating. There wasn't a safe way to explain what he'd done in regards to that. "I'm letting a friend of mine name him."

"Is this friend a short, cute blonde or the adorable daughter who comes with her?"

Gunner stared up at the sky in annoyance. "What did Gran say?"

"You know Gran. She said just enough and then clammed right up once I showed any interest in my brother's social life. Is this a *thing*?" Ellie drew the last word out with a twang that gave the term a dozen meanings.

"No, this isn't a thing. Audie's just some little girl who is all into bison. Her class is coming here later this week. I don't know what made me tell her she could name the little guy. She's in the third grade. I'll probably end up with something terrible like Rainbow Sparkle."

Ellie laughed, and Gunner smiled. Making Ellie laugh had always been one of his favorite things to do in the world. "You're probably right. Then you can call him Spark or some other manly derivative suitable for cowboy life. Call me if you get stuck—I am a communications professional, you know."

"So's her mom. She works for DelTex—the Ramble Acres people—so you can see why this *isn't* a *thing*." He gave the word Ellie's telltale drawl.

Gunner heard Ellie shift and sigh. "Speaking of things…" She paused a long moment before she said, "Kayla's getting married." When Gunner didn't reply, she added, "I figured you'd want to know."

Gunner kicked his legs out and sank back against the truck. "Yeah, well, it's not like I'll get an invitation, is it?" Gunner and Kayla had been a thing. A very serious thing. Only, as it turned out, the seriousness had all been on Gunner's side. The night he'd found her getting all cozy with some rodeo wannabe stood as one of the worst nights in his life. The only good thing about that whole drama was that Mama's ring hadn't yet made it onto Kayla's finger, even though Gunner had been only days away from asking.

"You're not mad I'm still friends with her, are you?"

Gunner was, but it wasn't his call to make. "It's a free country, Ellie."

"You two would have been good together, but she wasn't ready. I'm sorry you got hurt."

"Seems she up and *got* ready." He'd never told Ellie he had planned to propose to Kayla. He hadn't told anyone. Given his past, no one expected him to even think about settling down. He'd come to think of the whole thing as a bullet dodged, but somehow the news of Kayla's engagement jabbed under his ribs. "I'm happy for her."

"You are not. And I don't expect you to be. I just thought you ought to know."

"And now I know. Let's talk about something else. Things heating up between you and Derek? You planning on catching any bouquets at Kayla's wedding?"

He could hear the smile in her voice. "Could be. I always said I wanted to marry a man who cooks."

"I'm happy for you. And that's not a lie. Kayla, not so much, but you? You still have to bring this Derek out to the ranch soon so I can decide if he's good enough for you. He'll have to ask me, you know."

"You'd make Derek ask you for my hand in marriage? You're the last person I'd call old-fashioned."

"Protective never goes out of style." Daisy snorted and gave Gunner another look as if to say "Are you going to be talking long?" He rose off the truck. "I'd better get back to the house. Daisy's giving me looks."

"We can't have that. Hey, how is Gran? She says she's fine, but is she? Really?"

Gunner gave the corral gate a final check. "She's doing okay. Aches and pains, but still going strong. As a matter of fact, she wants me to take her to some whoop-de-do charity thing later this month for Senator Rostam. A black-tie gala. Can you see me at one of those? I told Gran I was sure she could do better with someone else."

"Still trying to make you into the community pillar Dad was, hmm?" came Ellie's amused voice. "Someone ought to curb that woman's optimism."

"I own a tux. I clean up just fine."

"You own *Dad's* tux, and you hardly clean up ever."

"Vintage tuxes are cool. I'll be fighting off grandmothers all night." His low laughter died down as he looked around the dark yard. "I miss you, Els. Feels weird being back here without you."

"Is that why you're resorting to grade-school field trips?"

"Community relations, Ellie."

He could hear Ellie's laugh over the phone. "You and a bunch of third graders—that's not community relations, that's a crime against nature."

Gunner quoted the Blue Thorn website. "'Blue Thorn Ranch has a commitment to community awareness. People who understand the bison will respect the bison and the land they need to survive.' You wrote that."

"And my public-relations heart beats a lit-

tle faster to hear you say it. Tell you what—
I'll see if I can get away before summer and
you can tell me all about Cowboy Buckton's
Bison Love Festival for Third Graders."

Gunner could just see Ellie putting the title
in air quotes with her fingers. "Save it, sister."

"You sure you're okay about Kayla?"

He wasn't. It bugged him twelve ways to
Sunday that she'd found some guy to settle
down with when he clearly hadn't made the
cut. But if that wasn't ancient history to him,
it needed to be soon. "I'm long over it, Els."
Maybe saying it enough would make it true.
He *wanted* it to be true.

"Okay, then. See you in a month or so if I
can pull it off."

"Bring Chef Wonderful with you when
you come. I need to check him out."

Ellie laughed. "Derek works weekends.
And I'm not letting you at him yet. He needs
to meet the Bucktons in small doses, and
probably you last."

"I'm wounded. And here I thought I was so charming."

"Somebody better warn those third graders, that's all I have to say. Good night, Gunner. My love to Gran."

Gunner clicked off the phone and stared up at the empty sky. He hadn't thought about Kayla in weeks. Months even. No, what surprised him most was how often the Calders had been creeping into his thoughts.

He liked Audie, and was growing to like Brooke, but the only influence he'd let the Calder women have over his life would be with Rainbow Sparkle, or whatever name that poor calf ended up receiving. "Knowing Audie," he said, staring back at the pen behind him as he recalled the girl's pink backpack and purple sparkle notebook, "I reckon by Friday I'll owe you an apology, little guy. You're done for."

Chapter Nine

Brooke closed her file and slid it onto Jace Markham's desk. "I've been out to the ranch a number of times. I haven't spoken to Adele a great deal, but I've spent considerable time with Gunner. It's going to be a long, uphill battle to get him to sell, sir."

"Well, that's no surprise to me. The whole point in you going out there is to work on softening him up. Or Adele—you should try and get in some more time with her. You said she likes you and your daughter. Make use of that."

Brooke didn't like the sound of that suggestion—she certainly wouldn't be using her daughter or the sweet relationship Adele had formed with Audie to close a business deal. But maybe Mr. Markham hadn't meant it that way. She moved on. "Gunner is convinced whatever offer he gets won't be fair. Are we prepared to spend a little extra money on this?" Brooke asked. "Maybe a lot of extra money?"

Mr. Markham frowned. "I'm hoping it won't come to that. That's why we are counting on you to smooth the way here. You say you're making progress."

"I'd say so, yes."

"Glad to hear it. I'll make sure those above me hear it, too. Make no mistake, Brooke, this could be quite a feather in your cap if you pull this off."

She knew that. "What if I can't budge him? Do we have an alternative? Surely this isn't the first time DelTex has come across a situation like this."

After pulling the file toward him, Mr.

Markham tucked it in a drawer. "I've got people working on that right now, as a matter of fact. But I don't think it will come to that. I have faith in you. You've already made more progress than I ever could, and it's clear those Bucktons have taken a shine to you and little…"

"Audie," Brooke offered.

"Little Audie. Do you have a picture?"

Brooke pulled out her phone and opened an adorable shot of Audie standing in front of the bison pasture. "Here she is, at the Blue Thorn, as a matter of fact."

"Isn't she a sweetie?" Mr. Markham handed the phone back. "Just keep doing what you're doing. It always pays to be on good terms with your neighbors, don't you think?"

Brooke felt a glow of maternal pride. Mr. Markham had never taken an interest in Audie before. Maybe she really was establishing herself at DelTex. "Isn't that why DelTex has a community-relations department?"

Mr. Markham laughed. "So when's the big field trip?" Brooke had told him the whole story about how Gunner had been coerced into hosting Mrs. Cleydon's class.

"This Thursday. I hoped to take the morning off and go with them, if it's okay with you."

"I've already told you to take all the time and resources you need to deal with the Bucktons. You don't even have to ask."

Brooke sat back. "But this is a class field trip."

He waved her concern off. "If you're on Buckton land, you're helping to serve our interest. When I said do whatever you need to do, I meant it."

Brooke felt it was time to ask, "If you don't mind my asking, what is DelTex's alternative to the Bucktons not selling?"

"Oh, there are several options we're working on. Believe me, we wouldn't bank a project as large as this on the compliance of a single rancher. Oh, I almost forgot." Mr.

Markham smiled as he reached into his drawer. "If you're looking to make some gains with Adele, I may have just the ticket. Literally." He produced two black shiny cards with gold embossed letters. "Senator Rostam is having a gala for one of his favorite charities this Saturday night. Lots of big players will be there, and we have a few extra seats at one of our tables. Adele might be there, too. I think you should go."

A gala? Brooke hadn't had to dress up for anything that nice in years. "Seriously? Me?"

"I don't think any of our younger staff has the grace to handle an event like this. I need a more dignified presence. And there will be a lot of people there who could help your career as well as DelTex. Think of it as a reward for the extra effort you've put in on Ramble Acres. I'm sure a single mom like you could use a fancy night out."

The last time Brooke had needed a baby-sitter, it had been nothing more exciting than a pizza and a pedicure. A fancy night out? On the company dime? There seemed no reason to say no, especially when it was her boss suggesting it. She took the tickets. "Thank you, Mr. Markham. I'd enjoy that." Then, as she stared at the pair, she asked, "I know it's an odd question, but is this something where I need a date, or can I come on my own?"

"Well, no one *needs* a date in this day and age," Mr. Markham said, even as he looked as though he didn't believe that for a second. "But I'm sure you'll think of someone to serve as your escort. Just make sure it's not Stuart." Stuart Higgins was the graphic designer on staff and a bit of a wild man. The thought of him at an event like this made Brooke cringe, and she could see why Mr. Markham had offered the tickets to her.

"It's black-tie. And if I know Nolan Rostam, the food will be fabulous."

What on earth will I wear to a black-tie gala? Brooke thought as she slipped the tickets into her file. "Thanks again. I'm sure it will be a wonderful evening." She looked at her watch. "So I'll just take the morning on Thursday for the field trip and be back for the three o'clock department meeting."

"No reason to worry about that. You take the whole day." He looked at his watch, as well. "That's right, you need to be heading out. We can go over the sales brochures tomorrow morning. No need to stay late."

It bugged her when Mr. Markham said *no need to stay late* like that. His tone always made her feel as if she was letting him down a bit by not choosing to stay late on her own accord. He never came out and said it, but there was a catch in his tone that belied his friendly words. A subtle reminder that he knew she was often the first one to leave at the end of the day. Then again, he'd just given her a massive perk in the gala tickets. That had to mean her position and contributions counted for something despite her tight time frames.

"I can stay late tomorrow if you need me," she offered. "Audie has swimming lessons, and she walks over to the pool with a bunch of other kids from after-school care."

"Nonsense. No need. We'll be just fine." Again, the *we* was a subtle reminder that several other members of the staff regularly ate dinner at their desks. Still, hadn't Mr. Markham just encouraged her to take a whole day off? Why should she let a few cutting remarks undermine the truth? She *was* pulling her weight—more than her weight, actually—and she didn't have to keep crazy hours like the others to do it.

"Those sales brochures will be on your desk first thing tomorrow morning." The brochures were some of her finest work to date—they made Ramble Acres look like the best thing to happen to Travis County. Because, in many ways, it was. Austin was growing like wildfire, but some of the more rural areas had yet to feel the boom. DelTex was going to bring hundreds if not thousands of jobs into the area and would have a fabulous impact on local property values. Audie's generation would know a different community—a more complex, vital, growing community where once only failing ranches had been clinging to a weak existence—thanks to the funds DelTex was pouring into the area. That was something families could appreciate, and her new campaign was going to excel at showing it to them.

DelTex built homes for families. Mr. Markham himself was a family man. Sure, it was harder as a single mom, but Brooke could show him how she balanced work and home. She *had* been showing him. One day she and Audie would move into Ramble Acres, and Audie would attend the state-of-the-art school that went with it. Their future had a bright horizon, even if now felt hard.

You are good at what you do. Mr. Markham makes snide comments about everyone, not just you. Your job is not on the line—you're on the fast track. You're in a position to make yourself invaluable here—take the opportunity and run with it. "Good, then." Brooke rose with confidence. Leaving at 5:30 p.m. was no crime and no weakness. "And thanks for the gala tickets. I'll see you in the morning."

Gran gave one of her long-suffering sighs over dinner. "I wish you'd have come to Sunday service this weekend, Gunner. You could do with a dose of church."

One of Gran's friends came over every Sunday to drive her to church, and it was always accompanied by some polite—and not so polite—arm-twisting to come along.

He offered his usual reply. "You know what Dad always said—it's better to be on the ranch thinking about church than to be in church thinking about being on the ranch."

She swatted him with her napkin. "That

only works if I believe you ever think about church."

"Those folks would just about fall over dead to see me walk in that door, Gran." Too many people in town still looked sideways at him for him to try anything as hypocritical as showing up in that stiff little white church with the hard wooden pews. He knew God was there, but Gunner had a ways to go before they'd get on closer terms.

"So don't go to my church. Go somewhere else. Go to one of them big fancy high-tech churches young people like these days. Ask Brooke where she goes—Audie told me she loves it there."

For a second, Gunner considered asking Gran how she'd already gotten to the topic of the Almighty with Audie Calder, but this was Gran. The woman never met a stranger. Everyone loved her and told her everything. It was one of the reasons the prospect of ever running Blue Thorn without her kept him up nights. He knew how prickly he was, how people didn't take a shine to him right away the way they did with Gran. He'd seen what Dad's sharp demeanor had done to the health of the ranch.

He silenced her by leaning in to kiss her cheek. "I love you, Gran, but you need to back off on this. I've got a lot on my mind."

"All the more reason to get your soul in the right place, boy."

Gunner groaned and took his plate to the sink. "Haven't I cleaned up enough for you?"

She came and stood behind him. "You've cleaned up plenty. And don't think I don't know how hard that was. I'm proud every day of how you've turned out. Takes a real man, a strong man, to turn around and face what's his to face." She grabbed his hand and shook it. "But there's more to life than work. I know it. You know it."

He grinned at her, helpless to be annoyed at the boundless affection and optimism

Gran had for him. "Are there gonna start being elbow marks on my bed again?"

"'Course not," she said, but before turning she added, "I can't get down that far at my age."

Chapter Ten

Thursday morning, Gunner could hear kids yelling and singing almost before the big yellow school bus came into sight. He stood among the gingham-checked picnic tables—Gran had outdone herself so much that he was a little worried about her—and felt his gut tighten. What had ever made him think this was a good idea? Surely no community awareness was worth the chaos the next two hours would bring.

"Children on the Blue Thorn!" Gran came up and tucked her arm into Gunner's elbow.

"It does my heart good to hear all that wonderful, noisy energy."

"It's noisy, and it's energetic, but I'll save the *wonderful* for after it's all over." He fought the urge to swallow hard as the sound grew louder. "Listen to that. And we're gonna give them lemonade and ice cream? Won't that just make it worse?"

Gran tugged on his arm. "You may surprise yourself by having fun today."

He gave Gran a dubious look.

"Although I do think it was a good call to keep Daisy and the calf out of this. Has Audie given you a name yet?"

"She's going to tell me today. She wants to do it in front of the whole class."

Gran smiled. "So everyone can enjoy the moment."

Gunner frowned. "Actually, I think it's so I can't back down. Poor little Rainbow Sparkle back there doesn't know what he's in for." He couldn't stop thinking of the doomed beast in terms of that silly name—and that bugged him immensely.

"She's not really going to use a name like that," Gran chided. "She's smart, that Audie. Besides, I think her mama's been coaching her."

Oh, that makes it all better, for sure, Gunner thought. "How do you know that?"

"Because Audie sent me an email yesterday saying she and her mama had been using a thesaurus to help pick out the calf's name. That's a book that—"

"I know what a thesaurus is, Gran." He was a bit impressed, but not prepared to admit it.

"Well, I don't know too many third graders who know how to use one, so I'm guessing Brooke's been in on the nominations. That ought to keep the rainbows and sparkles out of things. At least for a male calf."

Children were spilling out of the bus in squirmy groups of two and three. "Let's hope so." He was glad to see at least two adults climb out of the bus alongside the children, gladder still that one of them was Brooke. She caught his eye right away, and he couldn't decide what that meant.

"Well, here we are," she said, walking straight up to him and gesturing for the woman he guessed to be the teacher to follow. She tossed her hair out of her eyes, and he felt the motion tickle his stomach. He'd always been a goner for a great head of hair, and Brooke Calder had fabulous, wavy, golden-blond locks that looked even better today than the last time he saw her. "Mrs. Cleydon, this is Gunner Buckton Junior and his grandmother, Adele Buckton. We're here at their kind invitation."

Mrs. Cleydon smiled and extended her hand. "Thank you so much for having us. This is a wonderful opportunity for the children."

"I made sure there were no nuts in the brownies like you asked," Gran said as she shook Mrs. Cleydon's hand.

Brownies, too? She'll be scraping them off the classroom ceiling this afternoon, Gunner mused. He was glad he got them for education first, while Gran supervised the snacks afterward.

"You've really outdone yourselves," Brooke said, motioning toward the tables where the other adult was filing the kids onto benches. As the teacher walked back toward her class, Brooke leaned toward Gran and whispered, "You've made me classroom volunteer of the month, I think. I owe you."

"Nonsense. The whole thing was Gunner's idea."

Funny, I don't remember it that way, Gunner thought. "I've arranged for some of the feed bags to be put out over there in about fifteen minutes." He motioned to the rolling portion of pasture right in the children's field of view. "That should bring most of the herd right up to where the kids can see them. And I printed out a fact sheet for each of them." Mrs. Cleydon had suggested Gunner talk for about ten minutes, giving basic bison facts that were also listed on a paper where the children could write down key words in blanks. He'd felt out of his league making up a child's worksheet, but when the teacher had told him it was perfect, he'd felt a silly sense of pride. He could talk for hours on the amazing things about bison, but he'd never done it to an audience who barely came up to his waist.

"Welcome to Blue Thorn Ranch, children!" Gran had been assigned the official welcome, and the huge smile on her face tugged at Gunner's heart. Gran was always a bundle of vitality, but today—despite the huge number of tasks she'd set for herself—she seemed to light up with twice the usual glow. As he listened to her welcome, he saw the Gran he'd adored as a child—full of love and warmth and smiles. Despite all the tough spots in his life, even as an ornery and troubled teen, Gran had made him feel as if he had a special place in her world. He'd do anything for that woman.

Including play host to a gaggle of wiggly third graders.

"But before we go any further, I understand Audie has an announcement to make." Gran's voice brought his thoughts back to the present. "Why don't you come up here, dear, and explain to your classmates?"

If Gran glowed, Audie positively radiated happiness. The girl was grinning from ear to ear—a goofy, crazy echo of her mother's engaging smile. "My mom got to meet Daisy a while ago, and I got the special chance to meet Daisy's calf when he was born. They need to be alone for a while, so we can't see them today. But because Mr. Buckton is such a nice man, y'all get to be part of announcing the calf's name." Audie's chest puffed up with pride. "I got to pick his name. I thought long and hard and even studied a—" she worked to get the word right "—thesaurus to come up with just the right name."

Here it comes. Gunner braced himself, determined to show nothing but approval no matter what came out of Audie's mouth in the next ten seconds. He even caught Brooke flashing him a glance as if to check his reaction.

"I've given Daisy's calf the name Russet. It's a word for the pretty orange color he is right now. He won't stay that color—he'll be brown like his mama someday—but this way he'll get to keep the color with him his whole life."

Stunned didn't even begin to cover it. Not only had Audie picked a name that wasn't embarrassing, she'd gone and picked a downright brilliant name for the calf. One he *liked*. One he wished *he'd* thought of. Audie was looking right at him when she made the announcement, and he hoped his face showed more of the pleasure he felt than the shock currently echoing through his system. *That'll teach me to underestimate an eight-year-old girl*, he thought, nodding in such a way as to give Audie no doubt of his approval. When Gran started applauding, he joined in without hesitation.

"I'm sorry y'all can't see Russet and his mama today," Gunner announced as he walked over to stand next to Audie, "but new calves need to be left alone. We've got another animal that you'll get to meet up close later." The new name felt smooth and perfect on his tongue—just the right mix of rugged and artistic. Ellie would go wild when he told her the story. Ellie was always for anything that took Gunner down a peg; and getting his comeuppance from an eight-year-old would be just the icing on the cake for his kid sister. If Gran used a smartphone, she'd probably be texting Ellie in all capital letters this instant.

Gunner went through the worksheet with minimal chaos. He was interrupted twice with questions, but they were good ones, so he didn't mind. What made it hard to think, however, was the beaming look on

Brooke Calder's face as she sat in the back row of tables. A sweet, wide-eyed look that was half proud mama and half grateful female. Something about the way that woman glowed when she was happy—the polar opposite of the impatient, harried woman he'd met that first time on the road with Daisy— made him want to keep her glowing.

She's getting to me. The thought buzzed a certain spot under his collarbone. He would have preferred to ignore his pleasure at having her on the ranch again, but the truth wouldn't stay put. It crawled under his skin like an unscratchable itch.

I ought to leave her be. I ought to keep a wide distance between her and me, he scolded himself, reminding himself that Kayla had already schooled him well in what a conniving woman can do to a man. And he had double the reason to distrust Brooke, given her affiliation with DelTex. If he was smart, today should be Brooke and Audie's last visit to Blue Thorn Ranch.

As he left the children to complete their coloring pages—something to occupy them while he saw to the feed bags being set on the pasture to draw the bison—Brooke smiled. Gunner allowed himself a long, slow gaze of that sunny smile and knew he was long past being smart about those two. Audie and Brooke would be back.

It was one of the most amazing things Brooke had ever seen. The pickup truck rolled onto the hillside with two ranch hands sitting in the back, slicing open huge bags of feed to spill out of the truck bed onto the grass. At first one brown hump rose up over the ridge, followed by a small group, until what looked like a hundred bison thundered full tilt toward the truck.

Magnificent was the word that came to mind again, but she quickly paired it with *dangerous* as the hands stayed well inside the truck bed, out of the way of each bison's massive head and sturdy horns. She remembered how big Daisy looked up close. To be surrounded by so many, and when they were so hungry?

"They never leave the truck near the herd. No one's ever gotten trampled" came Gunner's voice over her shoulder. "One or two have come close, but only because they didn't take the animals seriously. You have to respect a two-thousand-pound bull or you may not live to change your mind."

"It's like a movie." Brooke shaded her eyes against the bright sun and marveled at the moving, grunting wall of brown fur encircling the truck. "An honest-to-goodness buffalo stampede." She turned to look up at Gunner. "Thank you. I mean, really, this is so much more than I was expecting."

He shifted back on his hips and adjusted his hat. "Gran tends to go all out."

His dodge of the compliment only charmed her further. "Gran did not arrange that spectacle for a bunch of eight-year-olds. Look at them. Even the boys are impressed."

"Well, then, my work here is done. Of course, Audie made it a mite easier for me by choosing such a fine name."

She'd seen his shock at Audie's announcement. "You were worried, weren't you?"

Gunner scratched his chin in a display of nonchalance Brooke didn't believe for one second. "Nah."

She poked his arm. "Yes, you were. What? Did you think she'd come up with some fluffy name you'd hate?"

Gunner shook his head, but he'd flinched just enough at the words *fluffy name* that she knew she'd hit it on the head. "What did you think you'd end up with?"

"I hadn't given it much thought." The smile hiding at the corners of his eyes gave him away. Brooke crossed her arms over her chest. "Okay," he admitted, "maybe I gave it a bit of thought."

Now she wasn't going to let him get away without a further admission. "What name did you think she'd give you?"

Gunner scuffed one boot on the gravel and lowered his head. "*Fluffy* about covers it."

"What? Buffy Bobbie Buffalo or something?" She'd actually worried about the same thing before the thesaurus session, given Audie's tendency toward pink, sparkles and ruffles, but Gunner's reddening neck told her he'd imagined much worse. She poked his arm again, suddenly aware that she wasn't acting much older than a third grader herself. "Tell me. I won't laugh."

That drew him to look straight at her. Goodness, but that man's eyes were blue. "Oh, you will. You'll fall over laughing and I'll be hung."

"Will I? Oh, now you have to tell me. Out with it."

He hedged, fidgeting a bit before stuffing his hands into his back pockets as if to shore himself up for the ridicule. She wasn't going to make fun of him no matter what he was about to say. She was nicer than that.

"Well, I was pretty sure I was going to

end up with something like—" he actually cringed, but with such an endearing smile that Brooke felt her heart skip a little "—like Rainbow Sparkle."

She'd told herself she wasn't going to laugh. He deserved her restraint after all he'd done for Audie and for the class. Despite all that, she burst out laughing, even though she'd covered her mouth with her hand.

"See?" he said, settling his hat down farther on his head as if that would hide a man of his size and presence. Several children turned to look at them, forcing Brooke to hide her laughter behind a mock cough. "That's exactly why I didn't want to tell you."

"Given Audie's love of rainbows and sparkly things, it wasn't a bad guess," she offered, feeling her cheeks turn pink even as she watched the color on his neck rise. He rubbed his neck as if he'd followed her gaze. "But I can't even fathom your brain coming up with anything like Rainbow Sparkle. It's hysterical, really." She recalled his deep voice saying the name with such a sense of embarrassment that she broke into laughter again. "I'm sorry, that's not fair."

"No, ma'am, it ain't fair." Now, at least, he was laughing a bit along with her. "Your Audie picked a fine name, and I'll thank you to keep my unfounded fears to yourself."

She owed him that much. "Your secret is safe with me. Russet will never know the bullet he dodged."

"Oh, he knows."

"You told that poor calf he could end up as Rainbow Sparkle? To his face in front of his mama?" It occurred to her there wasn't much logic in talking about a bison in such human terms, but lots of things about Gunner Buckton and Blue Thorn Ranch defied logic for her.

"I figure I owed the poor little guy an apology for what I thought I was letting him in for. Maybe the person I ought to fess up to is Audie. I doubted her, and she came through like a champ."

She looked over to the crowd of children watching the bison feed. Audie was talking excitedly to the group, relating everything she'd learned on her visits to the ranch. While Audie wasn't anything close to shy, she didn't take the lead at school very often. A glow of mama pride bubbled up in her to see Audie so engaged and confident with her classmates. "She is amazing, isn't she?"

She hadn't planned to say anything like that, and Brooke was pleased to see Gunner's face break into a warm smile at her boast. "I don't know what it is about that girl of yours, but you can't help but like her." He looked away from Brooke at that moment, making her wonder if he hadn't planned to say anything like that, either. It felt too possible that they were talking about more than just Audie. For a courageous second, Brooke thought about asking Gunner if he'd take the second gala ticket Mr. Markham had offered her. After all, it'd be a nice thank-you for all he was doing today. "Gunner," she began, tamping down her nerves, "would you…"

"Look, children!" Adele's voice interrupted their conversation. "Mr. Flatrock is bringing out a bison for you to meet."

The ranch foreman led a small animal out into the pen where Audie had first met Daisy. The kids rushed over to the fence, setting both Gunner and Brooke into a fast trot over to the pen to keep everyone safe. Billy and the bison were still a distance away, but Brooke remembered all the warnings about wild animals Gunner had given them on their first encounter.

He went through the same speech Audie had heard then about how bison weren't always friendly and how their size and strength could make them dangerous. As he spoke, Brooke watched him and Adele line the kids up against the fence in small groups. As Billy walked the animal by, he explained that this bison was also a bottle-raised orphan like Daisy. Gunner helped each one reach out and touch the soft brown fur. Gunner made a great show of how he wasn't much for kids, but all of that was proven wrong as she watched him interact. He talked *to* them, not *at* them, and the kids clearly caught his genuine passion for the animals and their welfare.

After their "up close and personal" as Adele called it, she led the kids to a basin and had them wash their hands before declaring it snack time. The appearance of ice cream and brownies sent the kids into squeals of delight.

"You'd think they never saw ice cream before," Gunner said, making a show of putting his fingers in his ears.

The enthusiasm was a bit deafening, but then again the bus-ride singing had been just as loud. "Usually it's just juice and crackers, I guess."

"Well, that's Gran for you. Over-the-top again."

"I think she's wonderful," Brooke admitted. And she meant it. Adele's rampant exuberance made the woman a joy to be around. It made her wonder how much of a grump Gunner might have been without someone like his gran in his life. Gunner struck her as capable of happiness, just wary of it. Losing Jim had given her a sort of radar for people with a hole in their hearts—a "takes one to know one" sense of other's scars. Certainly the loss of his parents and the rift with his father would have been enough to do that to a man, but it felt like more to her. Maybe that was why he hadn't yet married despite his land and his looks—for he had more than enough of both to catch any number of Texan fillies.

"She's something else, that's for sure." The two of them watched Adele in all her glory, flitting between children, accepting hugs and smiling back at ice-cream-and-brownie-smudged faces.

She wanted to make sure she said it. "Thank you. Really. This has been wonderful."

When he returned her smile, she saw a hint of his grandmother's vitality in his eyes. He was more like Adele than he knew—or would ever admit. "Believe it or not, I enjoyed myself." He leaned in, and Brooke smelled an intoxicating mix of leather and soap and cowboy. "Don't you dare tell a soul."

Chapter Eleven

Gunner adjusted his tie for the third time Saturday night, feeling every bit of the starch in his tuxedo shirt. There was a reason he didn't work in an office—he hated getting fussed up for things like this.

"Why are we going to this?" he called down the hall to Gran's room, where she was clearly enjoying getting all gussied up.

"People still do invite me to things, Gunner. I like to go, and Heartstrings is a fine and worthy cause."

She walked into the hallway, and even Gunner had to admit she looked wonderful. One glimpse at her in the sparkly silver dress she wore, and he could see why Grandpa had fallen head over heels. "Are you bringing me along for protection?" he teased. "You'll be fighting off herds of old cowboys looking like that."

She blushed, but her pleasure at the compliment glowed in her eyes. "I see you haven't lost your touch. My, but you do lay it on thick." She winked. "Keep it coming. At my age, I gotta savor every compliment."

"I like a good time as much as the next guy—" not that tonight qualified as anything he would consider a good time "—but Nolan Rostam's event? He's in tight with Jace Markham. I'm sure DelTex has a dozen tables at this thing."

"The whole world does not boil down to Jace Markham and his agenda." Gran adjusted an earring. "And even if he's there, it might be good for you two bulls to lock horns on neutral ground. I'd much rather face Markham in a fancy setting over a good meal than go through the unpleasantness of tossing him off my property."

Gunner fiddled with an uncooperative cuff link. Gran had a point, he supposed. While they'd tried all sorts of refusals, the one thing they hadn't done was to say a declarative "no" face-to-face. Maybe tonight would be the best place to drive the point politely home. Or not so politely.

"Here, let me do that." Gran settled the turquoise-and-silver-studded cuff link into place. They had been Grandpa's, and he saw the memory mist over her eyes for a moment. "I do declare, you look sharp." She giggled—a marvelous, velvety laugh he hadn't heard nearly enough lately. "Maybe it's *you* who'll need *my* protection tonight."

He rolled his eyes at the suggestion. The kinds of women who usually went to these things weren't his choice of companions anymore. The ones who weren't married were on the prowl—and quite frankly, so were far too many of the ones who were married. "I doubt that."

"Have you ever thought that Brooke might be there? She works for DelTex."

"I don't think she's high enough up to land an invite to something like this. She'd have mentioned it, I think."

"I didn't tell her we were going. Did you?"

"It never came up." The possibility of seeing Brooke settled ticklish in the back of his brain. "But I doubt she'll be there."

"You never know. Anyone could be waiting for you tonight, ready to show you a marvelous evening. That's the thing about these shindigs. You have to go *deciding* you're going to have a good time."

"Women love to dress up, I get it. If you had to wear one of these monkey suits, however, you might not be hankering to go so much." He ran his finger under the stiff collar. "They itch."

"If I can have fun in high heels, you can have fun looking like an oil baron. Half the men end up pulling off their ties after dessert anyhow." She looked at him, head to toe, a bittersweet smile turning up one corner of her mouth. "My, but you look like your father tonight."

He leaned down and kissed Gran's cheek. She'd even put on perfume tonight—she really was doing it up. "And you look beautiful, Gran."

She grabbed his hand. "Let's go show them the Blue Thorn has still got it, shall we?"

Forty minutes later, Gunner handed the keys to the ranch's shiny old Cadillac—Gran's car that hardly ever got used but was washed and waxed for the occasion—to the valet and offered his grandmother his arm. They walked through the grand old entrance of the Driskill hotel, as opulent a setting as Austin had to offer. The place looked like Texas's version of a king's castle—just the spot for a senator looking to make a fine showing before an election year.

Gran looked in her element, but Gunner

felt like a pretender. He may need to move in these circles someday if the Blue Thorn were to rise to its former glory, but today the whole exercise felt over his head. *A blue-jean guy invading a black-tie world.* Gunner found himself wishing Brooke really was here just so he wouldn't feel so out of place.

Gran pulled on his elbow as they found their names among the sea of place cards set up outside the ballroom. "When you see Jace Markham—and you will, I'm sure of it—you will be civil. You can be firm, but you'll be a gentleman about it, no matter how he pushes. Understood?"

"Yes, ma'am." It'd be hard, but he'd do it. Markham had a talent for pushing his buttons, but tonight he'd show Gran he could be the diplomat the Blue Thorn needed at its helm.

He was just turning into the ballroom when he saw it: a place card marked "Mrs. Brooke Calder and Guest." She was here. That thought sent a hum under his ribs and changed the atmosphere of the entire evening for him.

But she wasn't here alone.

That shouldn't be an issue for him, but the truth was he didn't welcome the idea of watching Brooke Calder dance and dine with some other man. The unfounded jealousy surprised and annoyed him. He didn't want to get personal with Brooke Calder, and yet part of him already had. The confused tightening in his gut was going to make it a long night.

Gran had followed his stare, for she touched the card with Brooke's name and slanted a sideways glance at Gunner. "See? She *is* here. Won't that make for an interesting evening?" She gave the word *interesting* a teasing tone, waggling one gray eyebrow to boot.

"She's with a guest, Gran." He tried to keep his voice neutral, but realized too late that his comment about her *guest* revealed his thinking. This was the last area Gran needed any encouragement to start meddling.

"So are you." She didn't have to say "and you're unattached"; her eyes shouted it at him. "Table sixteen. That'll be near ours, I expect."

Gunner picked up his and Gran's cards and scanned the number eighteen in one corner. *What fool placed us near the DelTex tables?* So now not only did he have to endure running into Brooke Calder all dressed up on a date with another man, he was in danger of having her in full view for most of the evening, too. The bow tie around his neck was starting to feel more like a noose.

He spent the next ten minutes trying not to look over his shoulder at the entryway while Gran glided from one group of friends to another, shaking hands and waving at everyone. Here was that same truth again on display in front of him: everyone loved Gran. He knew Gunner Buckton Senior was not as universally loved as Gran and Grandpa had been, but he also knew times had been harder when Dad took the reins of the Blue Thorn. Choices were tougher, resources tight and competition had made enemies of friends all over the region.

This was another reason he didn't go to church. People were cordial to him but always a bit suspicious, because of his own black-sheep past, and because of their problems with his father. At big events like this, Gunner always felt as if the whole world was still deciding whether or not to accept him.

Gunner's hand was starting to ache from endless handshakes when he caught sight of her. Over someone's shoulder, on the far side of the room, he picked her particular hair color out of the crowd. Her back was to him, a fortunate advantage as he stared at the creamy skin of her shoulders against a brilliant blue satiny dress she wore. When he noticed the wash of freckles on those shoulders, the room temperature seemed to rise a dozen degrees.

He didn't want to be caught staring when she turned around. Right now he held the advantage—since he'd picked up his table card before she arrived, he knew she was here, but she didn't know he was present. He was going to have to time their meeting carefully in order to keep that advantage. It was leverage and control he was going to need. He could already imagine what the color of that dress did to Brooke's eyes. In fact, he was having trouble thinking of anything else.

"Gran, would you like some punch or something before we sit down?"

She saw right through him, of course. She said a simple "Sure," but her eyes said *Are you heading toward her or hiding from her?*

"I'm thirsty, too," he replied, hoping his own eyes said *That's none of your business.* "I'll go get us some drinks."

Brooke couldn't have been the only woman here at the event alone, but it sure felt like it. Audie and the sitter had fawned over her choice of dress and hairstyle, telling her she looked lovely, but Brooke still felt like an imposter. The opulent ballroom was filled with people of wealth, status and power—this wasn't her world. She'd been let in as a prize for good behavior, and while that should have made her feel special and valued, it only made Brooke feel awkward and tolerated. *It's like a grown-up version of moving from the kids' table to sitting with the adults at Thanksgiving,* she thought to herself. *I'm here, but not like everyone else.*

Part of that is your own fault, you chicken, she scolded herself, and she picked up her place card, the words "and Guest" mocking her from the creamy card stock. Nothing had stopped her from bringing a date but her own fears and doubts. Even if it was a bad idea to ask Gunner—and it was, so she was glad she'd not followed through on that impulse—there were a few men from church and even one or two single fathers from

Audie's class that she could have brought to the gala. She still would have felt like the poor relation, but at least she'd have had company. *But you didn't, so now you're going to have to live with it. This room is filled with people who can help your career, so don't you dare leave early. You're smart enough and strong enough to handle this.*

Brooke gathered her courage as she fixed a stray curl in a nearby mirror. She remembered her mother's words that night after Audie's bedtime prayers, the first day she even began to admit she might be ready to let another man into her life. *You'll never totally be ready.* She'd told her mother Gunner was complicated. *Okay, Lord,* she prayed as she clutched her evening bag a bit tighter and turned toward the glittering crowd gathered around an elaborate punch fountain, *help me have an enjoyable evening. If there's a nice, uncomplicated man in that sea of tuxedos, I wouldn't mind You sending him my way.*

"Well, look here. You must be Brooke

Calder, only you don't look at all like the Brooke Calder from my office." Jace Markham gave her a huge smile as he nudged his wife. "Lorna, this is that young woman from our communications department I was telling you about."

"With the little girl," Mrs. Markham cooed. "Yes, I remember. You single mothers have got it hard, bless your heart."

Brooke was hoping for more of a professional compliment, and she'd heard *bless your heart* enough times in the past two years to last a lifetime, but she smiled and shook the jeweled hand the woman offered. "I enjoy my work at DelTex very much, Mrs. Markham."

"Well, I know my Jace thinks very highly of you. And he was just saying how very creative you've been with Adele Buckton and her lot over there at the Blue Thorn."

"Did he, now?"

It took a moment for Brooke to place the owner of the deep voice behind her. It took

another moment for her to catch her breath
when she turned to see Gunner Buckton in a
tuxedo. He looked exceedingly handsome—
and exceedingly peeved. "Gunner!"

"So you two *do* know each other." Mrs.
Markham seemed delighted at the unfolding drama.

Gunner Buckton and Jace Markham stared
each other down like a pair of bulls about to
charge. Brooke angled herself between them.
"Did your husband tell you what a wonderful field trip Gunner arranged for my Audie
and her third-grade class? Adele even served
them ice cream."

Her words did nothing to soften the dag-
gered looks flying between the two men.
Brooke flashed a "help me" look to Mrs.
Markham, hoping for any assistance in
preventing what was starting to look like
quite a scene, but Lorna Markham merely
smiled. "So you're Adele's grandson back
from wherever. I remember you when you

were just a little thing, but you've been gone a long time, haven't you?"

"I came home when it came to my attention the Blue Thorn needed defending." Gunner addressed that last word to Mr. Markham.

"It was just happenstance that one of the Blue Thorn bison blocked my way on the road coming back from Ramble Acres one afternoon. Gunner came to my rescue, and Audie and I have gotten to know the animal quite well, actually." Brooke was sure she was babbling, but she was too afraid to leave enough space for those men to go at it.

"I wasn't aware folks were so welcoming on the Blue Thorn," Mr. Markham said, tucking his hands into the pockets of the brocade vest he wore.

"Really, they've been wonderful," Brooke offered.

"Does me good to hear it," he said. "Maybe we can finally have that chat I've been meaning to have with you and your grandma."

"Maybe not," Gunner bristled, "and you'll

have it with me if you have it at all. Which you won't."

"Y'all are not going to be talking business on a night like this," Mrs. Markham scolded with practiced cheer. "I won't have my fancy night taken up with negotiations." She gave the final word an unpleasant tone.

"Now, Lorna, we're just being social." Mr. Markham held up one hand.

"You two are about as social as a pair of longhorns pawing the ground at each other." Brooke was glad when the woman tugged on her husband's arm. "Come on, Jace. I want to go say hello to Bo Davis and his new bride." She nodded at Brooke. "Nice to meet you, dear. Enjoy yourself tonight."

Fat chance of that, Brooke thought as she looked up at Gunner's sharp frown. "Was that really necessary?"

He ignored her question. "Why are you here?"

She didn't care for his tone. "My boss gave me tickets." Immediately, she wished she'd said something that sounded more like she had every right to be at a ritzy event like this.

"A prize for weaseling your way onto the Blue Thorn?"

Brooke hated that Gunner used the very word she'd thought of in terms of these tickets. "That's low, Gunner. I don't know what it's going to take to convince you Audie's visit was not some sort of setup."

"It's going to take a lot more time than you have. You ought to run back to your date now—he'll be wondering what happened to you."

"I don't have one." It jumped out of her mouth from sheer annoyance. She lifted her chin, determined to show strength. "I'm perfectly capable of attending a gala without an escort, thank you very much."

"So you couldn't land a date, either, hmm?" His tone was anything but commiserating.

"Oh, there you are, Gunner, I've been—" Brooke had been so busy steeling herself from Gunner's fierce glare that she hadn't even noticed Adele come up. "Oh, my stars, look who it is! Brooke, you look positively radiant. I had no idea you were coming to this."

"Yes, Gran, isn't it amazing how she keeps popping up in our lives?" Gunner shot her a dark look, but Brooke refused to flinch. "Who could have planned it?"

"I know Gunner was so pleased to see your name on the place-card table, dear. I'm sure he thought he'd be bored stiff being stuck with an old hen like me all evening."

Gunner didn't look anything close to pleased at the moment. It didn't take long for Adele to pick up on the tension. "Someone want to tell me who threw ice water on this party?"

"Markham." Gunner practically ground the name out through his teeth.

Adele looked at Brooke. "They didn't fight, did they?"

"Well, they came very close," Brooke admitted.

Gunner stuffed his hands in his pants

pockets. That cowboy cleaned up entirely too nicely—it would be a lot easier to stay annoyed at his behavior if he didn't look quite so eye-popping in that tux. "Brooke is here as a reward for getting on our ranch."

Okay, maybe not so hard to stay annoyed. "Stop that."

"DelTex is one of the corporate sponsors of Heartstrings and their programs for children. Brooke has every right to be here." Adele had to practically crane her head to look Gunner in the eye, but she didn't back down. "I told you not to rise to Markham's bait no matter what he said."

"Actually, Gunner started it." Brooke felt a guilty pleasure at calling Gunner out.

"Markham's wife was preening on about how *creative* Brooke had been to get on our land." Gunner's eyes were a mix of hurt and anger. How had this whole thing become such a tangled mess?

She had to fix this now—for both personal and professional reasons. *Words are my gift,*

Lord, she prayed as she took a steadying breath, *give me the right ones here.*

"If I explain myself, Gunner, will you actually listen?"

Chapter Twelve

Gunner was steamed. Brooke Calder had pulled the wool over his eyes, and he'd let her. He, of all people, should know not to let a pretty face hijack his good sense, and that made him as angry at himself as he was at Brooke. Still, this wasn't the place to make a scene.

He mentally counted to ten, eyeing her while pushing a breath out of his lungs and unclenching his fist. "Yes."

"Is there someplace a little quieter we can talk?"

"If I remember right," Gran offered,

"there's a little parlor down the hall. It's a half hour before we sit down for dinner. You two can go talk in there."

Gunner looked at his grandmother. "You're not coming?"

Gran planted her cane resolutely on the plush carpeting. "*I* don't need convincing." With that, she walked away toward a nearby knot of people as if nothing at all had dampened her evening.

Well, his evening was sopping wet. A washout if ever there was one. He stuffed his hands back into his pockets, torn between wanting to walk right out of the place and wanting to know just how Brooke Calder was going to explain herself.

"Well?" she said, nodding in the direction Gran had pointed.

"Ten minutes. That's all."

Brooke didn't flinch at his ultimatum. "Ten it is." She began walking toward the parlor. Gunner followed, barking orders to himself to keep his eyes off the way her dress glimmered in the hallway lamplight. He didn't know what that shimmery fabric was, but it ought to be illegal. That woman was a whopping load of frustration and fascination that just wouldn't go away.

He pulled open the parlor door for her, pleased to find a small, private sitting room just as Gran remembered. As the latch clicked behind them, Gunner cursed how his pulse registered the privacy, hiking up a rebellious notch at the prospect of being alone with this beautiful, infuriating woman.

She turned to him, determination lighting up her eyes. At this moment, angry as she was, her calm control showed her to be stronger than he'd ever given her credit for. It was the first time he considered the possibility that she was not the pawn of Jace Markham he'd thought her to be.

"You're right," she began, a new command in her voice. "DelTex is very supportive of me getting to know you and Adele. I have been asked to do anything I think might help open up a conversation. But that does not include *weaseling*—" her eyes glinted as she used his choice of verbs "—my way into you good graces.

"My job is to understand both sides so communication can happen. You want to keep the creek. DelTex needs to use that creek. Both sides are right."

Gunner leaned against a credenza, crossing his arms over his chest. He'd vowed to give her a full five minutes of silence before he responded to whatever she had to say— enough rope to hang herself, Dad would have said—so he merely nodded.

"But you have my word, on my honor as Audie's mother, that my first visit was motivated by Audie and her school project. Yes, I told Mr. Markham that I'd been to visit you. And yes, he did ask me to take advantage of that opportunity to build some lines of communication. But I did it as much for Audie as for DelTex. Actually, I did it for me, too. I've enjoyed getting to know the ranch. I want it to succeed. A standoff won't help that, will it? If there is a compromise to be had—" Gunner pushed off the credenza at the statement, but she held up her hand "—and I'm not saying there is, but if a compromise is possible, we will never know unless you *talk to each other*."

I finished talking to him long before you showed up, Gunner wanted to say, but kept his mouth shut.

"So yes, my boss is pleased to have someone from DelTex who can actually hold a conversation with you, but *you* should be pleased to have someone at DelTex who's willing to see things from your side—who cares about Blue Thorn Ranch. This isn't either-or, Gunner. I visit Blue Thorn because it's useful but also because *I like it there*. I like how Audie enjoys it, I think your grandmother is a marvelous woman and I respect what you are trying to do." Brooke tucked a curl behind her ear. "There are no professional reasons why I'll always be grateful for what you've done for Audie. Letting her name that calf made her feel like a million dollars, do you know that? It's such a tiny thing to you, I'm sure, but you have no idea what it means to her—and to me."

It wasn't a tiny thing. It was a huge thing he still couldn't explain to himself. It was part of the strange whatever it was that hung between them.

Brooke swallowed hard, and he watched her cheeks pink even as her emotions pitched her tone up a notch. "Your ranch? Your land? Even your animals? They're beautiful. More than I ever realized. I'm glad, I'm—" she tripped a bit on the word "—thankful you let us be a little part of it. It's been a long time since I felt like a real live member of the human race, you know? It's been so... hard...since Jim died. I muster up the energy because Audie needs me to but, well, grief doesn't let you do much more than just go through the motions."

Gunner had been expecting some slick,

well-crafted persuasion; he hadn't expected such an emotional speech from her. It left him without any response save silence.

Brooke began pacing the room. "Would I like to be the person who makes a deal between DelTex and Blue Thorn possible? Of course I would. It would mean a lot for my career, and I've got a little girl to care for." She turned to look at Gunner, and he felt the power of her eyes clear down to the pit of his stomach. "But if you think so little of me that you believe I would manipulate and deceive you, that I would help to steal what I know means so much to you, then I've been all wrong about the time we've spent together."

He was trying to think what he should say to that when she surprised him by continuing, "I almost asked you to be my date for tonight. I started to, back at the field trip. Can you imagine that? The truth is, I couldn't think of anyone I'd want to spend an evening like this with more than you."

The admission should have surprised him,

but it didn't. Because he'd been thinking the exact same thing. The fact was disconcerting when it was only him thinking like that, but it was downright dangerous now that he knew she'd had the same inclination. The whole situation seemed to be tilting into very unpredictable territory. Should he admit it? Or would that just make everything worse? He ought to say something, respond in some way to the gush of confidences Brooke had just spilled, but how? Gunner couldn't remember the last time he was so at a loss for words.

Brooke was wringing her hands together, talking faster. "I know it's beyond complicated, and it seems you and Markham can't be in the same county together, much less have a civilized conversation, but if you had any idea how it feels to even *like* the idea of spending an evening with another man after what I've been through—" her breath hitched, and he realized she was actually fighting back tears "—you wouldn't be such a stubborn mule. You could have at least *told* me you were already coming." She tossed her evening bag on the side table and sank down into one of the parlor chairs, her hand over her eyes.

Buckton, you're a jerk. Say something. "Look, Brooke, I..."

She shot up off the chair again, fidgety hands flailing in the air. "Boy, I really don't know when to stop talking, do I? Now would be a good time for me to run from the room, I think—"

Gunner caught her hand as she went by, and she froze with the contact. "Hey. Hold on there."

Brooke turned to look up at him, and Gunner's insides tumbled in twelve different directions. Every clever and sophisticated response evaded him, so he went for the only words in his head. "I want to believe you." He ought to let go of her hand, but he didn't want to. He'd wanted to touch her since that afternoon out by the creek, but hadn't because he somehow knew it would feel the way it felt right now. It would tear down all the carefully laid distance he'd put between them.

"You can. I won't lie to you."

He tugged on her hand. "But you'll try to convince me to change my mind about Ramble Acres."

She tugged right back. "Yes, I probably will. Can you handle that?"

His answer surprised him. "I don't know. Maybe I can. I'm a stubborn mule, remember?" His fingers interlaced with hers, even though he'd given them no permission to do so.

"Sorry about that. But you are, actually."

He smiled. "Family trait. Then again, you're no shrinking violet yourself. Pretty easy to see where Audie gets her nerve." His brain was trying to retrace their steps from argument to hand-holding, but at the moment it didn't seem worth the effort.

Brooke bit her bottom lip—something he'd

seen Audie do—and gave his hand a slight squeeze before sliding her fingers from his grasp. "So now what?"

"You know," he offered, running a finger under that insufferably itchy shirt collar, "I have no idea." And then, suddenly, he did. "Hey, Brooke, did I mention I'm going to that thing for Senator Rostam's pet charity next week?"

It took her a second to catch on to what he was doing, but when she did, her eyes sparkled. "Why, no, Gunner, you hadn't mentioned it. I'll be there myself, actually. Maybe we'll see each other."

"We might at that." He tipped his hat. "I'm at table eighteen."

"Well, what do you know? I'm at table sixteen." Her chin tipped up in playful defiance as she picked up her evening bag. "That's where all the mean people from DelTex are seated."

"You'd best watch yourself, then. It's a dangerous thing to dine with predators."

"More dangerous than ice cream with third graders?"

Going toe-to-toe with Brooke Calder sparked something inside him he hadn't felt for a long time. "'Bout even, I'd say. Scenery's better here, if you're asking." He gave her a look designed to let her know just how fetching that blue dress was.

"You clean up pretty good yourself, cowboy."

Gunner shrugged. "I hate this thing." He gestured around the room. "I hate these fancy parties. I'm here for Gran."

She stepped toward him, and he felt the loss of distance between them in more ways than one. "Would you have said yes? If I'd asked?"

"Yeah." His reply came out as more of a breath than a word. "I would've."

"Well, then, maybe the evening can be saved for both of us." She motioned toward the door. "Are you game to try?"

He opened the door, surprised to find himself hoping table sixteen was right next to table eighteen. "I believe I am."

Brooke didn't remember the food. She didn't remember most of dinner. What she did remember was the sense of Gunner's gaze on her back all through the meal as she made small talk with an assortment of DelTex junior executives. Mr. and Mrs. Markham were, of course, at a table filled with much higher-placed DelTex brass than she, so some smitten part of her kept waiting for Gunner to suddenly sit himself down in the empty seat next to her. She'd catch Adele's laugh in the noise of the room and think about what it would be like to sit next to those two in all this glittering candlelight.

She was still shocked at the admissions she'd made in that parlor. Why had she opened herself up like that? Everything she'd said was true, but revealing it made her feel as if Gunner held all the cards in their relationship.

Relationship? This wasn't a relationship— it was a personal and professional minefield. Something was going to blow up if they both weren't very careful. *Oh, Lord*, she prayed as she sipped her after-dinner coffee while a very earnest man named Ed from the permits department boasted about the winning record of DelTex's company softball team, *guard my heart. I've got to trust You know what's best here.*

The band started—the program advertised two sets of country swing music broken up by a live charity auction—and Brooke kept her eyes on her coffee.

"Care to?" Ed said hopefully, putting down his napkin while he nodded toward the dance floor.

"Come on," said a woman from accounting as she pulled her newlywed husband toward the parquet. "Ed's a great dancer."

"Oh, I don't know." Before she could put up any further resistance, Ed had guided her to the dance floor and spun her around.

Brooke wasn't much of a dancer, but Ed was quite good and more than encouraging.

"See?" the man said. "Not that hard. We're not all boring bean counters in the accounting wing, you know. I know who you are. You sent me an email last week asking for aerial photographs to use in some sales brochures."

"Oh, yes, Ed. Now I remember." Brooke tried not to be obvious as she looked beyond Ed's shoulder to watch Gunner take a turn around the dance floor with Adele. He looked so charming as he took slow steps to accommodate his grandmother, smiling and laughing with her. Every few minutes he would find Brooke in the crowd, locking eyes with such intensity that Brooke tripped more than once. After two numbers, Gunner deposited Adele back at her table, tapped Ed on the shoulder and said, "Mind if I cut in?"

"Buckton?" Evidently, even the permits department knew who Gunner Buckton was and why it was a surprise for him to come asking a dance from anyone associated with DelTex.

Gunner smiled and nodded. "'Evening."

Ed gave Brooke a look that said he was as worried as he was impressed. Brooke gave what she hoped was a "why not?" look to Ed as a slower, lazy jazz waltz wafted out over the dance floor.

As she allowed Gunner to sweep her toward the music, Brooke had the sense that they were crossing a line. There was a tremendous amount at stake here that didn't even have to do with DelTex or the Blue Thorn. Either one of them could name a dozen reasons why this was a risky idea.

"You shocked him," she playfully scolded as they turned a corner.

"I expect we're shocking a lot of people at the moment," Gunner said, scanning the room over her shoulder. Brooke hadn't expected him to dance well. Or to look so drop-dead handsome in a tuxedo. And while no woman with a pulse would fail to be charmed by those things, it was the man she'd talked with out by the back creek of the Blue Thorn that had truly stolen her affections. That was the man she wanted to be her date this evening: the man who had reclaimed his place and purpose in the world with such conviction.

"You're enjoying this," she teased. The glint in Gunner's eyes showed echoes of his rebellious past, the angry young man who'd chosen to thumb his nose at his heritage.

"I am," he replied, "but not for the reason you think." The intensity of his turquoise eyes made her feel as though she'd swallowed starlight. "So, as a community-relations professional, is there anything persuasive you'd like to say? I find myself in a remarkably receptive mood at the moment."

"Suddenly, I find I don't want to talk about real estate." She ought to keep the breathy, astonished tone out of her voice, but couldn't for the life of her think how.

He laughed—a deep, smooth sound that oozed confidence. "Surprisingly enough, I feel exactly the same way." His hand tightened a bit around her waist, and Brooke felt herself slipping off the edge of some imaginary cliff. It should feel scary—it was, in lots of ways—but it also felt like waking up again after years of numb sleep.

He broke his gaze and looked over her shoulder. "Your boss is staring."

They spun half a turn, and Brooke was able to reply, "So is your grandmother."

He grinned. "I didn't tell her a single thing about our conversation in the parlor. Not that she didn't ask twenty times. I expect she's dying of curiosity right about now."

"Why would you do that?"

"I love Gran, but keeping a secret from her is nearly impossible. I figure one hour of mystery is about the best I can hope for. Besides, I think she knows more than both of us put together, don't you?" He pulled her a little bit closer. "Should I dip you and send everyone into fits?"

"No!" she gasped as he tilted her just a bit off balance. "I don't have your talent for shock." The music shifted to a slower tempo, and she felt the pull of his charisma tilt her, as well. "I need to take this a bit slower than you."

Gunner toned things down for the next minute or so, dancing with her carefully before he asked, "Were you happy with him?"

Of all the questions to pose on the dance floor, she hadn't expected that one. She knew exactly what he was asking. There was no need to ask who. It felt wrong to bring up Jim here, now. Then again, perhaps it was the most honest and brave thing Gunner could do.

"Yes. We were very happy."

Brooke waited for the massive lump to rise in her throat, for her chest to pinch and the surge of pain to wrap itself around her. She felt the hollow ache of loss, but not the sharp stab of grief. It felt as if Gunner was holding her up, his arms offering protection rather than invasion. Brooke wanted to lay her head on Gunner's shoulder—and if not for the crowd of bystanders, she might very well have allowed herself that intimacy. As it was, she simply drew strength from his hand on her back.

"Not enough happy in this world, if you ask me. Does Audie remember him?"

Now, there was a question to raise a lump in her throat. "I make sure she does. I tell her stories all the time, show her pictures. We even have some videos I take out on Father's Day. Then, of course, I have myself a good cry after she goes to bed."

The music stopped, leaving everyone standing on the dance floor for a moment. Gunner looked down at her tenderly. "Do we need to go back to arguing about real estate now?" His softly teasing "I don't want to hurt you" tone unwound her heart more than anything else he'd done.

"No, I'm okay. Well, mostly."

He nodded toward the huge French doors that opened onto a nearby balcony. It was the perfect spot—away from the crowd but not too private. He guided her by the hand, and she happily followed.

Once out into the night air, Brooke wanted to make him understand how much she appreciated the respect he'd paid her by his honest questions. "Thank you. For daring to ask about Jim, I mean."

Gunner turned and leaned against the balcony railing, all lanky cowboy despite the crisp tuxedo. "Suddenly, I'm thinking I didn't do myself any favors here. If you like 'em upstanding and principled, I'm not going to come out looking so good."

"You don't think of yourself as having principles?" That surprised her—Gunner's sense of obligation to his grandmother, Blue Thorn Ranch and the bison seemed to drive everything he did.

"Not so much. Look, I'm sorry I brought

it up." He turned to look out at the splendid scene of Austin's city lights spread out
around them. "It's just..." His words dropped
off.

"No." She touched his elbow. All this was
so awkward and new, a scary-wonderful she
didn't know quite how to handle. "I'm glad
you did. He's a huge part of my life. Of Audie's
life. It's silly to pretend he's not there."

There was a small silence before Gunner
asked, "Is he here?"

She knew exactly what he meant. She'd
spent so much time thinking DelTex was the
big wedge between them that it hadn't occurred to her that Jim might be the true obstacle. She chose honesty. "I don't know."

He sighed. "When two male bison are interested in the same female, they fight it out.
Horns and blood and all—sometimes even
to the death."

She pulled back, finding that a gruesome
metaphor. "Are you saying you're ready to
lock horns over me?" Once the words had left

her mouth, she grimaced—her reply sounded as inappropriate as Gunner's statement. *I'm so bad at this*, she thought as all the wonder of their dance together tonight seemed to vanish into a series of fumbling missteps.

Gunner's face reflected the same awkward anguish she felt. She was thankful they weren't on display back on the dance floor. "I'm saying…" He wiped his hands down his face, reaching for words. "I'm saying I know better than to lock horns with a memory. You said it yourself, no one wins a standoff."

How had she ever thought of this man as distant and condescending? Gunner showed more wisdom and tender grace than half the men she knew. Attraction warred with caution, making her heart pound and twist at the same time—an overpowering sensation that made it hard to breathe. "So now what?" Why was she always asking that question in Gunner's presence?

For a heart-stopping moment it looked as if Gunner would lean down and kiss her. The thought terrified her—it felt like such a huge leap to even think about kissing any man since Jim. And yet so much of her wanted to feel that splendor again, to know it was possible again after all that grief.

He took her hand. "So now I think it's best if I say good-night and thank you, ma'am. I will enjoy your persuasion campaign. But know this, darlin'—I won't sell. Not now, not ever." With that, he kissed her hand even as he kept his eyes locked on hers. Despite the challenge in his words, somehow it was the perfect gesture. A kiss and yet not *the* kiss. He had stated his case right beside hers. Even more unsettling, he had known what she was ready for—and what she wasn't. "Thank you for the very fine dance, for being straight with me and for being here tonight. You know where I stand, I know where you stand. The rest we'll just have to figure out later."

He turned and headed back to the ballroom, leaving Brooke to grip the balcony rail until her breath returned.

Chapter Thirteen

Brooke wasn't at all surprised to find a note on her desk Monday morning asking her to come see Mr. Markham. She'd managed to restrict the conversation to small talk and leave quickly Saturday night, her thoughts too muddled to face his interrogation at the gala. Now, with the space of time and prayer, she felt better able to face her boss.

"I could ask you how your weekend went, but I have a feeling I already know," Mr. Markham said with a grin as she entered the office.

"It was a lovely event, Mr. Markham. Thank you very much for including me."

He rose and poured himself a cup of coffee from the credenza, holding the cup up to ask if she wanted one. In her career at Del-Tex, it was the first time he'd offered her coffee. "How about we dispense with the Mr. Markham business and you call me Jace."

All of Mr. Markham's colleagues called him Jace, but only some of his understaff had been extended the privilege. "Yes, Jace, I'd love some coffee, thanks."

He set the cups down on the front edge of the desk, choosing the second guest chair beside it rather than his usual position in the massive black leather chair behind his desk. "I take it you've made considerable strides in your relationship with the Bucktons."

She'd given some thought to how to answer that. "I would say I've grown closer to the family, yes. They're wonderful people. They've been very kind to Audie, as well."

"Well, now, that's gratifying to hear." He sipped his coffee. "As I said, I have always held Adele Buckton in the highest respect."

Brooke picked up the coffee in front of her. Her office had a coffee machine and a stack of paper cups, but Mr. Markham drank from china cups and saucers. "I'm sure you'd like to hear that I've been able to persuade Adele and Gunner to consider an offer from Del-Tex."

"Darlin', it would make my day. It would make my month."

"You'll be disappointed, then, sir. You're right, I have made considerable strides in getting to know the Buckton family. If I were to ever say that I have—" she chose her word carefully here "—influence over Gunner Buckton, it would be now."

"Delighted to hear it," Mr. Markham said as he leaned back in satisfaction.

Brooke took a deep breath. "But I can say with certainty that I don't believe an offer exists that could persuade Gunner to sell that land to DelTex. He won't sell. Not to you, nor I imagine, to anyone. In my opinion, DelTex would be better served looking at other options."

Mr. Markham's frown was to be expected—he wasn't a man who liked to be disappointed. "In your opinion." He gave the words enough of an edge to let her know he hadn't asked for her opinion.

"My job involves nurturing DelTex's relationship with the community. If you press the Bucktons any further, I believe it will backfire on Ramble Acres. To be painfully honest, you'll cross the line from developer to corporate bully, and I think the consequences of that aren't worth whatever it is you had hoped to gain from that creek."

Mr. Markham took another long sip from his coffee. That man wielded pauses like a weapon—the silence unnerved her, as it was clearly meant to. "Ms. Calder, we were prepared to pay a big hunk of money for that creek for a very good reason. The options you referenced are expensive and time-consuming." He got up and walked to the chair behind his desk, effectively declaring the "friendly" portion of this meeting over.

Brooke had expected his disappointment, but the encounter was fast slipping into a dressing down she hadn't anticipated. "What I needed," he continued, "was for you to deliver their cooperation. And from what I saw Saturday night, Gunner Buckton was looking very cooperative." He leaned over the desk. "Now, you look to me like a woman who knows how to put an advantage into play. May I suggest you play your advantage here? You are in a particular position to be of vital use to this company. We reward our vital players, Ms. Calder. We reward them very nicely."

Of that Brooke had no doubt. But for the first time since being hired on, Brooke was rethinking her desire to be a vital player for the likes of Jace Markham. What good was

a bunch of financial advantages if her conscience paid the price?

Her alarm must have shown on her face,
for Markham sat back. "Now, don't misun-
derstand me. I'm not suggesting you do anything unprofessional."

Aren't you? Brooke wanted to reply. *Isn't
that exactly what you're suggesting?*

"No one wants this business with the Blue
Thorn to come to unpleasantness. You and I
have both agreed in the past that a compromise is our goal here."

"Yes, sir. But I'm telling you, Gunner
won't compromise. Not on this."

"Well, you said your little girl is cozy with
Adele. Can't you work on her?"

Work on her? "Even if she were inclined—
which I'm nearly certain she isn't—she
wouldn't cross Gunner."

Markham spread his hands on his desk.
"Well, then, Ms. Calder, I suggest you do
whatever is necessary to convince the both
of them." It was the closest thing to a threat

she'd ever heard from the man, and it made her blood run cold. If she didn't need this job so much, she'd be updating her résumé tonight. She might need to update it anyway, given how things were looking.

"I mean no disrespect, but this isn't really my department. Land acquisition? Sales negotiations? All that's a far cry from public relations."

"It became your job when you became the only member of DelTex to win an invitation onto Blue Thorn land. We agreed you would use that invitation to our advantage."

Markham obviously viewed their initial conversation way back after Daisy's stand-off in the road in a very different light than she had. "I agreed to let the invitation open up possibilities. What you're asking seems a rather different level of pressure."

"Not pressure, Ms. Calder, persuasion. And persuasion is very much your department."

She had to ask, "In the name of persuasion,

sir, what exactly are the alternatives DelTex is considering if the Bucktons won't sell?"

"Now, that truly isn't in your wheelhouse. You leave that to the legal and government-relations teams. No one wants you to get involved in anything that's going to get ugly." Brooke noticed he hadn't said *might*, he'd said *going to*. With a decidedly unpleasant edge. "But if you are looking for incentive, let me say directly that it would be far better for the Bucktons and everyone—" by which he clearly meant *for you* "—if we did this the friendly way. Like you said, no bullying."

Did he just threaten my job? Brooke blinked, unable to absorb what she thought she'd just heard. Sure, Markham was no warm and fuzzy guy, and he could be demanding of his staff, but this seemed to be a whole other level of slippery territory.

"Now," he said, as if they'd simply moved on to the next item of business, "when will those brochures of yours be ready?"

Brooke churned through the next four

items of business with her mind in tangles. How was she supposed to react to a meeting like this? Had Markham been merely unpleasant, or had he veered into unethical? On the surface his words crossed no lines, but his inflections? His insinuations? They seemed to shout "get a yes from Gunner or clear out your desk" loud and clear.

Her heart wanted to walk right out the door and right onto the Blue Thorn to tell Gunner trouble was coming. This wasn't the kind of message to deliver over the phone or in a text, and an email was definitely out of the question. Only, a visit wasn't an option, either. It was ten thirty in the morning and too much of a drive to try to pass it off as a lunch-hour errand. Even at the end of the day, there wasn't nearly enough time to get out to the Blue Thorn and be back in time to pick up Audie.

As she walked back to her desk, Brooke could think of only one option that her heart, her conscience and her boss could swallow.

She pulled up Gunner's cell number in her phone and typed Come for dinner tonight?

Gunner had just come in from installing a new fail-proof latch on the northwest gate when his cell phone beeped with an incoming text.

Come for dinner tonight?

He had intentionally left the next move up to Brooke—half because he thought she needed to set the pace given his declaration, and half because he didn't himself know what the next move ought to be.

He was staring at the screen when he noticed Gran at his side sneaking a peek. Feeling a schoolboy's urge to hide some note passed in class, he tilted the phone toward his chest and gave his grandmother a narrow-eyed look. "What's got you peeking?"

"Maybe the question ought to be 'what's

got you grinning'?" Gran's smile was teasing but kind. "As if I even need to ask."

"Text messages are private." Gunner thought he ought to at least try to put up a defense, pointless as it was.

"Waltzing in front of half of Austin is not. If you wanted to stake your claim on that woman, I expect you succeeded." Gran filled the teakettle and set it on the stove. "And I haven't asked about it, have I?"

Gunner nearly laughed at the pronouncement. While Gran hadn't asked a verbal question, she'd been teeming with curiosity the whole ride home and all day Sunday. "But you sure enough wanted to." He shouldn't have enjoyed keeping her in the dark like that, but a man couldn't squander the rare chance to stump the legendary Adele Buckton, now, could he?

She planted a hand on one hip. "How much longer are you gonna hold out on me, boy?"

Gunner sat down, ready to talk about it— needing to talk about it, as a matter of fact.

"Yes, I like her and it's mutual. And complicated."

Gran waved away the facts. "*Pshaw.* Simplest thing there is." When Gunner shot her a look, she amended, "Well, maybe not always. But I sure hope you're not going to let that business with Ramble Acres get in the way of something good."

Gran had hit the issue right on the head— or at least part of the issue. "I want to think there's a way through this, but I can't see it. It's a mess."

"What did she tell you in the parlor? Y'all sure looked like things had changed when you came in for dinner at the gala."

How could he describe the whole slew of emotions Brooke had shown him then? Her honesty deserved some privacy, but he wanted to make Gran understand. "I believe her when she says Markham didn't put her up to the whole bit with Daisy and Audie and even the field trip. She said it was partly professional but mostly personal—and all her own doing."

Gran sat down at the table, resting her cane against the chair back. "And you didn't believe her before?"

No sense lying now. "No."

"Well," Gran sighed, "I suppose you've earned the right to be gun-shy on women and truth." She looked at Gunner. "But don't you let what Kayla did to you paint your whole world with suspicions. Sounds like she's being honest. Brooke isn't Kayla. Not by a long shot."

"You thought Kayla was good for me, too." In truth, Gran had been highly in favor of his relationship with Kayla. She'd been as hurt by Kayla's betrayal as he was—almost.

"I did. But a person can be wrong without being wrong all the time."

"I want to get to know her better. She's—" he struggled for a way to describe what he found so attractive about Brooke Calder that didn't sound syrupy "—smart. Clever and strong. I mean, after what she went through with her husband, she'd have to be strong to survive."

"You know that better than anyone. You've had to be strong to get by with all you've lost, too. Makes sense to me that you'd understand each other." Gran leaned in and placed her thin hand on top of his, her pale skin and blue veins looking such a contrast to his large, tanned hand. "A woman of faith would be a good thing for you, Gunner. You need grounding. Strong ain't the same thing as solid. A man with a little girl in his life needs to be solid."

That was the other thing. "Audie," he said—sighed, really. "Then there's Audie."

The teakettle whistled, and Gran rose to fill her teapot. "I like that girl. She's something special, she is. I think Russet is as fine a name as we've ever given any calf, don't you?"

"Beats Rainbow Sparkle, that's for sure."

Gran laughed. "Oh, Ellie told me about

that. I'm glad she told me after the field trip or I would never have been able to keep a straight face." She turned after placing the lid on the pot to steep. "You connect with that little girl. That's something. It's a big something, if you're asking my opinion." She returned to her seat. "*Are* you asking my opinion?"

Gunner scratched his chin. "Yeah, I suppose I am."

Gran smiled. "Don't you be eating dinner here tonight. That's my opinion."

"I was letting her make the next move. I'm not sure she knows if she's ready. Maybe I'm not even ready. Audie, DelTex, there's a lot at stake here, Gran."

"I think she just showed you the next move. And, honey, no one's ever ready. And there's always a lot at stake. If it's meant to be, you'll find your way through the tricky parts. Maybe even be stronger for them— who knows? Your father once showed me a list of eleven reasons why he shouldn't marry your mother. On paper, ranked, even."

While a ranked list of pros and cons sounded exactly like Dad, Gunner hadn't heard this story about his father. "So what happened?"

"I asked Gunner if there was a reason *to* marry her. He said he could only come up with one—that he loved her and he felt like a better man when he was with her."

Dad had always said that. *Your mother made me a better man.* Trouble was, Dad could wield that phrase like a sledgeham-mer—*a better man. Straighten up, Gunner, be a better man. A better man wouldn't have done that, Gunner.* "What did you tell him?"

"I told him it was all the reason he needed. All the reasons not to marry someone are just problems to be solved if the one you marry makes you a better person. What you get, when you have someone like that, is a stronger pair to solve all those problems than either of you are alone. That's what God had in mind. That's the way it ought to be."

"Did Grandpa make you a better person?"

The answer showed in her eyes long before she spoke the words. "By far." She wiped a tear from her eyes and drew in a breath. "I expect that tea's ready by now."

Gunner watched her as she poured herself a cup of hot tea and then poured a glass of iced tea for him without even asking if he wanted one. He smiled as he pulled out his phone and typed back a reply to Brooke's invitation.

I'd like that. I can be there by 6.

He had a million things to do—and not much time if he was going to head in toward Austin and have dinner with Brooke—but he could carve out time for a cool drink with his grandmother.

Gran had just set the drinks down at the table when the phone rang. She turned to lift the receiver off the wall, peering up close at the screen—Gran still found caller ID wondrous but a bit sneaky. "Oh!" she said, eyebrows raised in astonishment as she held the phone to her ear. "Well, Nolan, what a surprise to hear from you."

Gunner had to piece together the conversation from the half he heard. "We had a lovely time, yes.

"Well, I suppose that's true.

"Oh, yes, I saw." That remark earned a wink as she looked at Gunner. His dance with Brooke must really have raised a few eyebrows.

Gran's expression changed. "What's a special entity? Don't speak legalese to me, Nolan, talk plain.

"You can't be serious.

"I thought they couldn't do that kind of thing anymore.

"Well, are you going to put a stop to it?

"Of course I have a lawyer. You recommended Ashton Palmer to us, don't you remember?"

Gunner felt his pulse increase. Senator Nolan Rostam and Gran had butted heads a few times over the years, but they still remained good friends. He'd seen them laughing with each other at the gala. What he was hearing now sounded like the beginnings of a whopping argument.

"I don't agree. I don't know how you could think I'd ever agree. Quite frankly, I think you're showing a lot of nerve to even call if you're not going to help us fight this.

"Owe me? You don't owe me this. You get no points from me for being the first to announce a war.

"Yes, it's a war, and as far as I'm concerned, this means you're on their side. Goodbye, Senator Rostam." She hung up the phone. "And good riddance, you treacherous old goat!" she yelled to the receiver.

"Gran, what?"

"That was Rostam." Her hand was shaking.

"I got that. What'd he say?"

"He thought he owed us the courtesy of an advance warning. DelTex has somehow gone and pressured their government cronies to invoke eminent domain." She grabbed the counter. "Gunner, they're taking our land."

Chapter Fourteen

Gunner's hands were white-knuckle gripped on his steering wheel as he took the freeway exit for the outskirts of Austin where Brooke lived. It seemed DelTex had abandoned its plans to buy Gunner's land and was now working behind the scenes to somehow pull government strings. Now the state was doing DelTex's dirty work, initiating eminent domain. How they'd convinced the government that his creek represented "water access needed for the public good" was beyond him. He only knew it opened doors for the state to forcibly remove the land from private ownership. A process that spelled the beginning of the end.

No, he wouldn't lose the whole ranch yet—only the creek and however much land around it DelTex had convinced the state to take—but it wouldn't stop there. Gunner knew of far too many instances where what started as one sliver of land became the whole property soon enough. Budget-starved municipalities welcomed tax-generating developments like Ramble Acres and their promise to transform struggling ranch lands into fancy growth and prosperity. Ranchers could fight eminent domain, but they hardly ever won. And the fair compensation the state would offer for the land they took would be anything but *fair*.

He thought about texting Brooke to say he wasn't coming. Or phoning her. Or simply never speaking to her again. Truth was, he wanted the satisfaction of seeing her face when he told her Senator Rostam had given them warning. He wanted to make her admit to his face that she'd set him up just as he suspected. His only regret, as he pulled into the driveway of Brooke's charming little house, was that he wasn't sure he could control his temper sufficiently in Audie's presence. She didn't deserve to hear what her mother had done to him. To his land. To the future of the baby bison she'd just named.

The whole business boiled in his gut as he rang Brooke's doorbell. When she pulled the door open, looking a bit upset, he felt it like a punch to his gut. She knew. She'd known all along. How could he have been suckered in by a pretty face again?

"Hi." Her smile didn't reach her eyes.

"Is Audie here?" They'd have it out on her front lawn if it kept Audie from hearing the accusations bursting to get out of his head right now.

"A friend invited her out for barbecue at the last minute. I'm glad because—"

"Because I have a lot to say to you right now that I don't want her to hear."

"You do?" She looked surprised. Wow, she was good. A real community-relations professional.

"Can I come in? Since Audie's not home, I really don't want to do this on your doorstep."

She pulled the door open. "Do what? What's going on? What do you know?"

It struck him as odd that despite all his anger, he noticed the warm and cozy atmosphere of her house. Audie's toys—pink sparkly things and a scattered collection of dolls and stuffed animals—were all over the little house. He felt like the proverbial bull in a china shop as he stood in her living room, as if one slip would allow his temper to explode and break something.

Brooke stared at him. "Gunner, what's wrong?"

He had no patience for pretense. "How long have you known about DelTex's plans to get the state to declare eminent domain on my land?"

"Eminent domain?" She sat down, looking suitably confused. "The county has invoked eminent domain on your land?"

Getting a fact wrong was a slick touch—she was good. "The state. Your buddy Nolan Rostam had the decency—if you can call it that—to call Gran and warn her what was coming. Really? Couldn't *you* scrape up enough decency to warn me? I thought we were going for honesty now."

Brooke ran her hand through her hair. "The option," she said, more to herself than to him. "That's the option."

"So you admit you knew? Do me the courtesy of dropping the act, would you? I think you owe me that much."

"Markham called me into his office this morning. He gave me some song and dance about how pleased he was that we'd 'gotten cozy' and practically threatened me with my job if I didn't convince you to cooperate. Well, you or Adele—I don't think he cared how I did it."

Gunner had always thought Markham a snake, but the guy had found a way to sink even lower in his opinion. "So it's been all about getting me to sell, all along? All that talk of finding a compromise? How could you stand there and put up such an act? How could you use Audie?"

"No! That's not how it is."

"Really? Well, then, how is it?" He was sickly curious how she'd couch her deception, what carefully crafted explanation she'd foist on him now.

"I admit, Markham was pleased we were getting close. I told you we talked about trying to open a conversation with you and Adele. I did want to avoid a standoff—I told you that, too."

"Oh, yes, you were all big eyes and charm and 'I love Blue Thorn.'" He'd bought it, too. Before the phone call, he'd made his mind up to kiss her tonight, to take things to the next level. Perhaps God really was watching out for him that he found out the truth before he'd done anything so stupid.

"I told Markham this morning that it couldn't be done," she said. "That you would never sell, that there wasn't an offer they could ever make that would change your mind." She started pacing again, the way she had in the parlor at the gala. Gunner hated how his mind cast back to the way he'd fallen for her in that room, drawn in by the vulnerability—or the pretense of vulnerability—she'd shown him. This would be so much easier if he felt hate, but all he felt was hurt. Burning, wounded hurt.

"He said something about options. That DelTex had options if you wouldn't sell. I asked him what they were, but he wouldn't tell me. I thought they were other properties, or something they could do to the development site. I never thought they'd go as far convincing the state to invoke eminent domain."

"You expect me to believe you never con-

sidered just how far DelTex would go to get
what they wanted? Don't you have any idea
who you work for?"

"Markham's never been that way with me.
Sure, he's no softie—he's always been demanding—but he's never threatened me with
my job before. He scared me this morning. I
asked you here because I wanted to let you
know I was worried about what he might
do."

*Come have dinner at my house so I can
lay out my boss's evil plan in person?* Not
likely. "No point in worrying, sweetheart,
it's already been done. It has to have been in
the works for a while. You and I both know
eminent domain is a no-win option for the
ranch. I was sunk from the start, and you
knew it all along, didn't you?"

"No." Her voice caught on the word, a stab
he felt under his ribs. "I always believed there
was a solution. At least I did, until today."

"There always *was* a solution. Markham
just used it."

"That's not what I meant. I always believed there was a compromise. I even thought—" she turned from him, softening her voice as she picked up the stuffed bison Gran had given Audie from where it sat on the couch "—that maybe God had placed me in this spot so that I could make that compromise happen."

If God thought the solution to this mess was Brooke Calder, then Gunner had a word or two to say to the Almighty about His choice of tactics. "You really thought there was an ending to all this where everybody wins?" He didn't know whether to admire her optimism or chide her foolishness. Or even believe a word coming out of her mouth. "You've got another think coming, that's for sure."

He hardened himself against the tears he saw welling in her eyes. "I never wanted this to happen. You have to believe that. I never thought DelTex would find a way to just take your land."

"I'm glad you see this for what it is—Del-Tex taking my land. Oh, the state will do the taking and they'll pretend to 'compensate' me with some ridiculous amount that doesn't even come close to what that land is worth—even if you could put a price on what's been in my family for three generations—but it won't ever be anything but robbery to me." He sat back on one hip, determined to get his say in fully before he walked out that door and never came back. "And a few years from now some other part of the Blue Thorn will become 'necessary for the public good' and they'll convince the state to steal that, too. Pretty soon there won't be enough land to sustain the herd, and by the time Audie's in high school Blue Thorn Ranch will be just another subdivision." He looked Brooke square in the eye. "*That's* who you work for. That's what's coming. You'd better fire up your way with words to find some way to explain it to Audie that lets you sleep at night, 'cause I don't think I could."

He started walking toward the door, pretty sure he couldn't stand to be here much longer, when she caught his elbow. "I haven't lied to you," she said, and he turned to watch a tear spill over her brimming eyes and slide down her cheek. "I meant everything I said at the gala. All of that is true."

Gunner stared down at her grip on his arm until Brooke's face reddened and she pulled her hand away. "Tell me the truth, Brooke. When you called that second time, was it really for Audie or to cozy up to my family on behalf of DelTex? The *truth*, if you'd be so kind. I think I'm entitled to that much."

Two more tears slid down her face, and her breath shuddered as she exhaled. He gave her this much; she looked him straight in the eye when she whispered, "Both."

"That's it right there, Brooke," Gunner said as he turned toward the door. "You can't have both."

* * *

Brooke felt the slam of the door as if a brick wall had fallen on her. She stared after the closed door for a long moment before curling into a ball on the couch with the stuffed bison in her lap and giving in to tears. If God was kind, she'd cry herself out before Audie came home. Then she'd take a hundred deep breaths and find some way to explain to her daughter why they probably wouldn't be visiting little Russet anytime soon. Or ever again.

How could she walk into work tomorrow morning, knowing that DelTex had orchestrated eminent domain, and probably had been planning that as a last resort all along? Could she work for a company that consumed private land like an afterthought, as if taking away a rancher's land was acceptable collateral damage in the name of upscale development?

She'd deceived herself. She'd ignored little warning signs; she'd believed and even written passages about the worthwhile trade-offs of development. She'd allowed herself to think of the Blue Thorn problem—as Markham liked to refer to it—as just a disagreement over a slice of land and a small creek. Only, Gunner was right; it wouldn't stay that way. She'd seen the long-range plans—DelTex had visions of three more large communities in the area. Once they had succeeded in securing eminent domain with the Bucktons, they wouldn't save it as a last resort the next time. Bigger developments needed more drainage—the problem of water rights would feed on itself, growing larger and needing more resources.

She couldn't bring herself to believe Blue Thorn Ranch was doomed. It couldn't be inevitable that Blue Thorn and its bison must eventually give way to condominium communities. She didn't want to think of herself as part of a system that destroyed what she'd seen on that sunny afternoon beside the creek with Gunner.

She didn't want to believe she was the cause of the searing hurt she'd just seen in Gunner's eyes. It wasn't just "we lost this battle" she saw in his eyes; it was "you did this to me." *I never meant it to come to this. I thought there was some other way. How can I make him believe that?*

With a hollow shudder, Brooke realized she couldn't. Her heart knew better, but the facts would never line up any other way than how Gunner saw them. She'd walked onto Blue Thorn land as a woman ready to turn a coincidence into a professional accomplishment, and ended up as a woman captivated by a man and his steadfast purpose.

There is no solution. There never was. I couldn't convince Gunner to sell because he shouldn't ever sell. Only, now he'll have no choice. She buried her face in the toy bison's fur, the particular scent painful and condemning against her cheeks. *I've lost my heart and now I might lose my job.* The delicate balance of progress she'd built up over the past year would come crumbling down tomorrow—had started already. Brooke pictured herself going to Oklahoma, her tail between her legs, having to start all over a third time. It felt more than she could bear.

An hour later, Brooke splashed water on her face in the kitchen sink and forced normality into her eyes as the front door opened. Audie came barreling through the door, still slurping through the straw of a take-out cup from the local barbecue chain. "Hi, Mom. I ate a ton of barbecue, and Mrs. Taylor even let us get pie for dessert. I'm stuffed."

Brooke managed a smile at the smears of barbecue sauce and blueberry on Audie's shirt. She was always of the opinion that messes meant fun, but the current mess of her life felt anything but fun. "Good for you. Any homework?"

Audie rolled her eyes. "Spelling. It's the worst."

"It's important." She accepted the now-empty cup and deposited it in the trash. "But I think you need to take a shower first. You're sticky just about everywhere."

Audie found a smear of pie on her finger and licked it off. "Worth it."

"Did you thank Mrs. Taylor?"

"Yes, Mom," Audie moaned as she plodded down the hall toward her bedroom. How could a third grader look so much like a teenager some days?

"Good manners are as important as spelling," she called as she pulled a new set of towels out of the linen closet. While Audie showered, Brooke threw away the chicken she'd had roasting for her dinner with Gunner—it had overcooked and been sitting out for too long while she sat on the couch in tears. She hadn't eaten anything yet. While yogurt would have been a good choice, she irresponsibly drowned her sorrows in two slices of the apple pie she'd bought for dessert. She felt bad enough to eat four slices, but that would cause more problems than it solved.

Audie came out in her pajamas—pink-and-purple stripes with ruffles all over the collar, cuffs and around her ankles—looking like a bedtime princess with her wet hair dark and curling around pink cheeks. "Can we go visit Russet this weekend?" she asked as she pulled her spelling folder from her backpack.

Brooke was hoping this wouldn't come up until at least tomorrow. "We'll see, baby."

Audie frowned as she climbed up into a kitchen chair. "*We'll see* always means *no*."

Brooke sat down opposite Audie. How could she explain today to an eight-year-old? "Well, you're right, it might be a while before we get to visit Russet."

Audie made a face. "But Grannie Buckton

said we could come visit anytime we wanted.
I want to see how much he's grown. Mr.
Gunner says he grows fast. What if I miss
him growing?"

Brooke opened the spelling folder, hoping for a distraction. "I'm sure you want to
visit Russet, and I'm sure Russet wants to
see you." She held up a worksheet. "Is this
the list we are supposed to be working on?"

Audie nodded, pulling a blank sheet of
paper from the stack Brooke kept on the
kitchen table for homework use. Audie stuck
out her tongue in consideration as she se-
lected a colored marker from the cup beside
the stack of papers—every shade of pink and
purple imaginable, some of them scented or
with glitter in the ink. She suddenly changed
her mind. "Oh, I forgot." She fished in her
backpack until she pulled out a colored pencil in a plastic baggie. "Mrs. Cleydon gave
it to me in art class. It's russet."

Brooke felt her stomach turn to knots—

and it had nothing to do with too much pie. "So you have a new favorite color?"

"No, I still like pink and purple best, but it's fun to have this, too."

Focusing on the list to dodge Audie's wide, happy eyes, Brooke read the first word. *"High."*

Audie wrote down the word. "Can we go to Blue Thorn anyway, even if we can't see Russet?"

Brooke sighed. There'd be no avoiding this, no matter how much she would have liked to put it off a few days. *"Every."*

Audie wrote it down, forgetting the second *e.* Brooke took a breath and began. "Mr. Gunner and I had an argument today, Audie. A very big, very grown-up argument."

Audie looked up at her. "And you're mad at him?"

Brooke went back to the list to buy her a moment to think. *"Near."* After Audie wrote, Brooke went on. "It's more like he's mad at me. My company did something he didn't like, something he thought was mean, and he thinks I am part of it."

"DelTex was mean to Mr. Gunner? How?"

Brooke pointed to the list. *"West."* Audie wrote. "It's too complicated to explain. But it has everyone sad and angry, and it might mean we don't get to visit the Blue Thorn anytime soon. I'm sorry about that, really I am."

Audie put down her pencil. "You'd never be mean to Mr. Gunner, would you?"

"Not on purpose, no. But sometimes big companies have to do things one person doesn't like. No one is happy that it happens, but sometimes there isn't anything you can do about it. I wish DelTex didn't do anything mean to Mr. Gunner, but I don't really get to say whether or not it happens. Your next word is *dress.*"

Audie picked up her russet pencil and wrote the word, putting a little heart next to it. "I like dresses." She looked up at Brooke. "Can't you tell your boss not to be mean?

Isn't part of your job to make people like DelTex? Is that why Mr. Gunner is mad at you?"

Brooke set down the paper. "It isn't that simple. And I'm very sad Mr. Gunner is mad at me. I like him a lot, and Grannie Buckton, too. I want us to stay friends, and I hope we can be, but it might take a while."

Audie slid off the chair and climbed into Brooke's arms. It took every effort Brooke had not to let the tears return as Audie snuggled down, still damp and soap-scented from her shower. "This is one of those big patience times, isn't it, Mama?"

"Yes," Brooke sighed. "Yes, it is."

Chapter Fifteen

"I don't recall asking to see you, Ms. Calder." Mr. Markham didn't even look up from the file he was reading.

"You got the state to pull eminent domain on the Bucktons. Did you ever even plan to have a discussion? Or was I just a convenient last-ditch campaign to make it look like you'd tried everything else?" If she was going to get fired, Brooke didn't see much point in mincing words.

"Now, let's not be harsh. Shut the door and sit down. Let's try and talk this out like the adults they pay us to be."

Brooke knew that tone. She'd heard it at too many public zoning hearings not to recognize it. Markham used it when he had won his point but still thought it worth his while to appear open-minded. For all she knew, he'd already spoken to human resources, and she'd be clearing her desk by lunchtime.

She shut the door. She sat down. But she made no effort to avoid sounding harsh when she spoke again. "I don't know what DelTex did to convince the state to launch eminent domain proceedings on the Buckton land, but it had to have been in the works long before yesterday. I think you pulled the trigger on it the minute I walked out of this office."

Markham steepled his hands. Brooke had to admire how eerily calm the man was— she was so worked up she couldn't even pour herself a cup of coffee this morning. "I hadn't planned for that information to get out just yet. I would have pulled back if you gave me any indication that the Bucktons would bend. I had hope after what I saw at the gala." He took off his glasses and looked at her. There was no anger in his face. Annoyance perhaps, disappointment, even, but not anger. "But yesterday you gave me no reason for optimism—even you can see that."

"Why bother pressuring me, then?"

"Because, Ms. Calder—" he rose and went to the side table for coffee, pouring himself but not offering her one "—I dislike playing the bully. Contrary to what you may think at the moment, I do care about how Del-Tex looks to the public. And besides, getting a government to use eminent domain is an expensive thing. We have to call in a lot of chips to make it happen."

"You told me you had other options."

"I told you we had alternatives that were not your concern. And I do recall saying things could get ugly. I'm sorry they did." He sighed as he sat down again. "I'm sorry Nolan felt he had to get all noble on us and fire a shot across the bow before we were ready. Yes, I heard about his phone call. It gets my attention when my first call of the day is Adele Buckton breathing fire. I hope to have that woman's spirit when I'm her age."

Brooke couldn't put it off any longer. "Are you going to fire me?"

"I have always liked your directness. No. Not yet. But I'll be watching how you handle this. We all have to swallow things that don't taste good in this business, Ms. Calder. It's not a skill everyone can learn."

It's not a skill I want to learn. Were she young and childless, Brooke might have walked into Markham's office, resignation in hand. She didn't have that luxury with Audie in the picture. And if she could put off having to retreat to Oklahoma—uprooting Audie from her home and her friends—if she could hang on here long enough to find someplace else to work, she would. "I don't like what we're doing here."

"No, I don't expect you do. Did you genuinely like Gunner and Adele?"

Brooke couldn't believe he even had to ask. Did he think what he saw at the gala was an act? Did he think her capable of all those visits to the Blue Thorn purely as DelTex community relations? Worst of all, did he think her capable of using Audie for such an end? "Yes, I did. I do."

"Well, then, I suppose I'm sorry all this has cost you that relationship. And your little girl—Adele told me she'd named one of the Blue Thorn calves. Adele's not taking this well at all, as you can imagine."

Brooke could imagine. It was bad enough to have Gunner believe the worst of her, but to have Adele believe it, as well? It made Brooke ill to think of it.

"I expect either she or Gunner will be calling the papers at some point. We'll need some press releases drawn up, but you can understand how I might think it best to have someone else handle that."

She would never want to write that press release, but even so, it added insult to injury to know Mr. Markham was now shifting work off her desk. Work he didn't think she was capable of doing properly. She'd get to keep her job—for now—but her career at DelTex had been effectively and permanently stalled. It was exactly what she'd told Gunner at the gala—*in a standoff, everyone loses.*

"Is there anything else, Ms. Calder?"

There wasn't anything else to say. "No, sir."

Brooke rose and walked slowly back to her cubicle. DelTex was ensuring that Gunner would lose his land, and no amount of fighting would stop it. Had she never met Daisy, had she never set foot on Blue Thorn land, she would have probably considered the whole thing a sad and regrettable but inevitable consequence of progress. *When did I become the kind of person who could think that way?* On the one hand, she was glad she'd not become some sort of callous company executive, but on the other hand, caring hurt. Right now it hurt a lot.

"Ed from Permits sent these files over," the staffer in the next cubicle said as he looked at her quizzically. "Something about aerial shots for the sales brochures?"

Sales brochures. That would be her life from now on. She was off the fast track, and while that stung, it didn't sting half as bad as the look in Gunner's eyes.

I can be okay with sales brochures, she told herself. *At least it's not running to Oklahoma. It's safer, and maybe safer is good.*

Brooke pulled open the interoffice envelope, a stack of black-and-white aerial photo prints with a Post-it note telling her digital versions had been sent to her by email. She tried to smile at the thought of friendly Ed from Permits and his surprising dancing skills, but thinking of him just brought back all the wonder of that night at the gala. Two of the aerial shots were wide enough scale that they even showed the back of what had to be Blue Thorn Ranch and other neighboring lands.

Brooke ran her finger down the road that bordered Gunner's ranch, tapping what looked like the spot where she first met Daisy. With a lump in her throat, she made out the creek running up on the north edge of the land, the creek that started this whole battle. She followed the wandering blue line until it came to the parcel of land that would be Ramble Acres. Would she be able to see that creek when she and Audie lived there? *If* she and Audie still got the opportunity to live there? Ramble Acres was slated to be an upscale community, and perhaps people who worked only on sales brochures wouldn't make the cut.

I'll never get ahead. I'll never be able to give Audie everything she deserves. But what she needs most is a mom who isn't ashamed of what she does, and I have that. Please, Lord, don't ever let me lose that.

Absentmindedly, Brooke let her finger follow the creek down along the back of the Blue Thorn, under the little bridge she'd crossed just before meeting Daisy and down through the neighboring rancher's land.

Where it stopped.

The photograph didn't stop—it went on for what must be another mile, but an area of the photograph lost its image. She looked at it closer, wondering if there was a smudge on the lens or clouds blocking the view.

There wasn't. If she wasn't mistaken, the image had been altered. Blurred out.

There were lots of reasons to blur an aerial photograph—if there were identifiable people or vehicles in the shot, or an animal carcass, or any number of things. None of those would be as large as the blot in this photograph. Brooke looked at another photograph and noticed the same blur in exactly the same place—and the timestamp on that photograph was a different day, so it wasn't people or animals needing to be removed.

What was it, then? And why was it smack-dab on top of the creek everyone was fighting over?

Brooke shifted over to her computer, bringing up the digital images. They contained the same issue. When she used her photo-viewing program to zoom in on the image, it was clear the photos had been altered. Someone wanted to make sure no one saw whatever was on the creek right there.

She closed the image files, feeling her pulse jump. Could there be another reason why that creek was so important to Del-Tex? Only, if that were true, why pressure Gunner and his family instead of the neighboring ranch? This other ranch was even downstream of Gunner's land, which made no sense at all.

Before she could talk herself out of it, Brooke copied the images onto a small jump drive and tucked it into her handbag to look over tonight. Something wasn't right.

Sweat poured down Gunner's back as he thrust the posthole digger into the earth Wednesday morning. There were machines for this sort of thing, but right now he needed someplace to put all the anger boiling up inside him. Making deep holes in the ground somehow fit his mood. It felt as if all of Blue Thorn was teetering on the edge of some deep hole, and three generations of Bucktons on this land were going to come to an end on his watch.

He wiped his brow with the hem of his T-shirt and pulled back to sink the double-bladed device into the ground again.

"Your daddy used to do that when he was good and mad, too."

Gunner hadn't even noticed Billy come up behind him. He looked up as he twisted the digger to create the round hole.

"I know all about what happened," Billy said, his black braid bobbing as he inclined his head toward the creek.

"Talked to Gran, did you?" Gunner yanked the digger and its hunk of sod out of the ground, depositing it by the side of the new hole.

"More like Miss Adele talked to me. When

she's mad, she talks. When you're mad, you dig. A lot of talking and digging going on this morning."

Gunner pulled a turquoise bandanna from his pocket and wiped his face. "How do we fight this, Billy?"

"*Are* you going to fight this?"

That seemed a crazy question—who wouldn't fight this? The Blue Thorn belonged to him. It belonged to his siblings, too, he knew that—but today it felt as if the whole battle rested squarely on his shoulders. It didn't matter that ranchers almost never won eminent domain battles. Did it?

Gunner looked out over the land, feeling such a burden for it that it felt as if the herd's largest bull was standing on his chest. He'd been so bent on leaving this place once, and now he couldn't imagine life anywhere else. "I can't just let it go." And then he dared to say the thing that had been eating him alive since the drive back from Brooke's last night. "Maybe if I'd have never left, if I'd have stayed on and been here when Dad was going downhill, it wouldn't have gotten to this."

"And if you had never come back, maybe it all would be worse." Billy reached down and plucked a blade of the tall grass. "Maybe if you had not brought the bison onto the ranch, it would have died much sooner."

Billy's words didn't calm him; they only burned in Gunner's throat. "The Blue Thorn isn't going to die. I won't let it. They might win the battle, but you and I both know it's a whole war. I won't go down without a fight. They may snatch the land out from underneath me one lousy sliver at a time, but I won't make it easy for them."

"And they will not make it easy for you."

Gunner sunk the posthole digger again. "Do you think I care about how hard they make it for me?"

Billy leaned back against the truck Gunner had driven out here. "I think you care

290 The Texas Rancher's Return

about a lot more than bison and land when it comes to what happened."

Gunner did not want to have this conversation. He didn't reply.

Billy grunted. "Rainbow Sparkle? Really?"

Gunner pushed up off the blade handles and threw his hands in the air. "You've gotta be kidding me." Did the whole ranch know about that now? He turned to Billy. "Who told you?"

"Miss Ellie. I heard your grandmother laughing on the phone with her the day after the children visited. But before that, I watched you with the children. Well, with one child. And her mother."

"She sold us out, Billy. And I invited her in." He picked up the digger again. "I knew what she was doing, and I let her go right on doing it."

"And what was she doing?"

"Getting under my skin so DelTex could steal my land. All her talk of *conversations* and *compromises* and *no one wins a stand-off.* Easy talk for someone who has a government land grab in their back pocket."

"She has called the house twice today. Your grandmother saw her name on the screen and wouldn't pick up the phone. Has she tried calling you?"

Gunner had turned off his phone. If Gran needed him, she could send Billy out here to find him. Anyone else he didn't care to talk to right now. He wanted the whole world to leave him alone. He pulled the soil up, dumped it out of the digger and walked over to where the next hole was needed. "She can call here twelve times a day for the next hundred years for all I care. Gran's not gonna take any of the calls and neither am I. And another thing—I'm giving the calf another name."

"I don't know. Russet is a fine name. I like it. He likes it."

Gunner was in no mood to debate whether

or not Russet liked his name. "That name doesn't get to stay."

"You want to go back to Rainbow Sparkle?"

Gunner swallowed the urge to hurl the clod of dirt by his feet at Billy. Instead, he pointed at the man with the darkest look he could muster. "Not one word. Ever again. Don't try me on it, neither." He sank the digger blades into the ground. "I'm thinking Thorn. Thorn fits."

"A painful name." Billy pointed to his chest. "Pain right here, hmm?"

Gunner wasn't quite sure he was ready to admit to anyone how much Brooke's deception had hurt him. To think he had invited it, had left himself open to another humiliation at the hands of a pretty face, galled him as much as DelTex's greed. He'd believed Brooke's claims of honesty. He'd even entertained the notion that they might be something special together—she was so smart, had seemed so sweet, and anyone could see that she connected with the land and even the animals.

That was what made her lies all the more hard to swallow—she'd convinced him she believed in what Blue Thorn stood for. And he'd bought it—hook, line and sinker. No one who *truly wanted what was best for everyone* would stand there and talk compromises while her bosses pulled the kill switch on his future. He should have seen through her act. He shouldn't have allowed himself to start caring about her the way he had. "Something like that," he mumbled to Billy without looking up.

"She hurt you."

Billy's three words sent a wave of pain across Gunner's chest. He simply nodded.

"Do you think she meant to hurt you all along?"

Gunner was tiring of all these questions. He moved on to the next hole, half hoping Billy wouldn't follow him. They could talk about this until the sun went down, and it wouldn't change the outcome headed his way. The end had begun; she'd launched it, he'd allowed it and now no one could stop it.

Gunner stopped digging for a minute. Did he really believe Brooke meant to hurt him all along? The facts lined up that way. But there was some stubborn part of him that wouldn't accept that what had grown between them was just an act. There was something there, something that came through loud and clear at the gala. It just didn't square with everything else that had happened since then. And when in doubt, he'd learned to assume the worst. He wiped his forehead with his sleeve. "Yeah," he said, as much to himself as to Billy, "I think she did."

"Could be true. Then again, if she means to hurt you, why is she still calling?"

Billy's prying was starting to get really irritating. "How should I know? Maybe she wants to rub it in."

The walkie-talkie hanging from Billy's belt chirped, followed by the scratchy audio of one of the ranch hands. "Hey, Billy, you with Gunner?"

Billy pulled the device from his belt and pressed the button. "I am. What's up?"

"There's a lady at the gate with a little kid. She's asking to come in, and she ain't taking no for an answer."

Billy looked at Gunner. Gunner looked at Billy. "You want me to send her away, boss?" Billy asked. "Or do you want to make good and sure she's only here to rub it in?"

Chapter Sixteen

It was a risky tactic to show up at the Blue
Thorn gate with Audie in tow. Brooke knew
that. She had no business calling in sick to
work and keeping Audie out of school today
to do what she was about to do, but this was
the only plan she could think of right now.
Besides, Audie hadn't stopped asking about
Russet, no matter what explanation Brooke
offered. If there was even the smallest possibility this would work, Brooke wanted to
give Audie one last chance for a visit with
the calf. No matter how angry Gunner might

be, she felt she could trust him not to blow up at Audie.

"He said he was coming out here," the ranch hand said from his side of the locked gate where Brooke stood while Audie sat in the car. Was Gunner coming to let her in or ensure she stayed locked out? It seemed as if hours until a pair of trucks drove over the pastures toward the gate.

The Gunner she'd seen in a tuxedo had been a dashing sight, but this Gunner— the dusty, lean-muscle cowboy in jeans and boots with a T-shirt sweat-damp and cling-ing to his chest—was the one who truly took her breath away. This Gunner was real. Grounded. Authentic.

And furious. If they ever made a colored pencil called "angry blue," they needed to use the way Gunner's eyes looked as he glared at her through the gates.

"Just when I think I've seen it all…" he growled.

"I have something you need to see."

"Oh, I've seen all I want to see from the likes of you."

Brooke knew this would be hard. She knew he'd put up a fight, maybe not even agree to see her. She'd been praying for the tiniest bit of consideration from him the whole drive out. If there was any chance she'd found what she thought she'd found, she'd endure his rage. This chance to make it right was a long shot, but she was willing to risk it to know she had tried everything. It was the only way she could walk away from this whole mess and still sleep at night.

"You need to see this." Brooke looked over Gunner's shoulder to send a pleading glance toward Billy. "Billy, he needs to see this."

She thrust the large manila envelope through the gate bars just as Audie yelled, "Hi, Mr. Flatrock!" from her car window.

"Hello, Audie!" Billy called in a friendly voice that gave no hint of the tension bristling between her and Gunner. He waved at

Audie, but sent a "tread carefully" look to Brooke as he stood behind his boss.

Gunner didn't take the envelope. "Give me one good reason why I should look at anything you give me."

"Because maybe—just maybe, I'm not sure—the way to fight Markham and Del-Tex is in there."

"And you'd hand me a way to fight your boss. You expect me to believe that after all that's happened?"

That man could be so stubborn. "No, I don't expect you to believe me. But I do expect you to look at the photos in there and believe them."

Gunner gave her a long, suspicious look before he took the envelope and undid the metal brad to slide out the two photographs Brooke had printed out last night.

He instantly recognized the aerial shots. "I know what my land looks like."

Brooke had to reach through the bars to point out the blurs she'd seen at her desk yesterday. "Look there." When she could barely reach the photos, she grabbed at the metal gate and said, "Can't you just open up? I promise I won't go ten steps onto your land."

Gunner grunted, looked at the photos again and gave a small nod to the ranch hand, who promptly punched a series of numbers into the keypad beside the gate.

"Hooray!" Audie called from the car, misunderstanding the gate opening as an invitation to pay a visit.

"I'll go talk with her," Billy offered, walking through the gate before Gunner could reply one way or the other.

"Here's the thing." Brooke moved forward, determined to state her case before Gunner tossed her and Audie off the property. "These shots have been altered. This part here—" she moved cautiously closer to Gunner to point to the spots that had been blurred out "—is smudged on both images. Now, sometimes we blur out cars or people or animals but the same spot is hidden on both photos taken three weeks apart."

"Why should I care how you doctor your sales photos?"

"Because look." Brooke held the two aerial shots side by side. "Look at your creek in this one from February. Now look at your creek in the one from earlier this month."

"I know my creek is running high. The mud is what stuck you in front of Daisy. Or so you claim."

"Look again. Look at the creek on your land, and then look at the creek on the other side of the blurred part." Brooke shot up a prayer that Gunner would see what she saw, that he would come to the same conclusion she had: that the photo had been doctored to hide a dam.

She could see the moment Gunner saw it. He held the March photo closer, squinting at it, something between a growl and a curse escaping his lips.

"The blurred-out spot isn't on your land.

You told me the road I was on divided your land from another rancher's. That other rancher was damming up the creek that runs from your land to his, mostly affecting the part on your side. Only, that makes no sense—I need you to help me figure out why."

"I know exactly why," Gunner said, starting toward his car. "Come on up to the house. Gran needs to see this."

Come on up to the house. Brooke took in those words like oxygen. It should have frightened her—she was possibly handing the Bucktons ammunition to fight her employer. What she had just done would certainly toss her job out the window. But from the moment she'd looked at those photographs on her laptop, the stranglehold her conscience had been keeping loosened up. When she'd asked Jim once why he took such risks in fighting those warlords back in Chad, he'd said because it was the only choice that let him breathe. It had only worried her back then, but she understood it now.

"Are we going to see Russet?" Audie's face was all smiles as Brooke got into the car.

"I sure hope so," Brooke answered. In the yard beside Daisy and Russet's pen would be the perfect place for Audie to be while she, Gunner and Adele worked out what the photos showed and what to do about it. "Mr. Gunner and Grannie Buckton and I have adult things to talk about, but I'm sure Mr. Flatrock would take you to see Russet. Maybe there are some other calves that have been born, too."

"Adult things. You mean make up from your fight."

Some days Brooke wondered who had hidden the eighty-year-old wise woman inside her eight-year-old daughter. "Well, hopefully that, too." Even if a reconciliation never happened—and she realized as the car pulled up the drive how very much she wanted it to happen—she could *breathe* knowing she'd done everything she could to save the Blue Thorn.

Adele's expression was blank but her eyes were too full as she came out onto the porch. Anger, disappointment, surprise, curiosity—they all seemed to be there in the old woman's expressive eyes. "Well, hello." Her words were flat and cautious. Markham had told her that Adele Buckton was no one to tangle with lightly, and today she could see why.

"Brooke brought us something that might help with DelTex."

"Help with DelTex?" Adele said, eyes narrowed in suspicion.

"You need to see this."

"Billy," Brooke began as Audie climbed out of the car, "do you think…"

"Hey, Audie, you don't want to listen to these grown-ups talk about grown-up stuff, do you? Wouldn't you rather go out by the corral and see how much Russet has grown?" The foreman gave an unusual emphasis on Russet's name and shot a funny look toward

Gunner when he did. Brooke wondered what that was about, but didn't think now was the time to ask.

"Sure!" Audie cheered, heading off with Billy without a single look back.

Brooke mouthed a silent "thank you" to the man as she watched Audie slip beside him and take his hand as if they were long-time buddies. *Please, Lord, don't let this be Audie's last visit to the Blue Thorn. Or mine.*

Gran had every right to look confused as Gunner led her and Brooke into the kitchen and spread the pair of photographs on the table.

"These are aerial shots DelTex took earlier this month and in February," Brooke explained. "I asked the permitting department for them last week in order to make some sales brochures. When I saw them yesterday, I noticed something."

"Look at the creek running between our land and Larkey's," Gunner said.

"You mean the one DelTex is stealing?" Gran never was one to mince words.

"Yeah, but look at it in this photograph and then again in the later one."

Gran peered. "I don't see whatever it is I'm supposed to see."

Brooke pointed to the altered spot. "Someone has intentionally blurred out part of the photograph on one spot. On multiple photographs. Now, often we blur out a private car or animals or things like that on an aerial shot, but it shouldn't have to happen over multiple days unless there's something else there—something permanent."

"Something DelTex doesn't want anyone to see," Gunner added. "It's a dam."

Gran looked up. "A dam? Why? Larkey needs that water same as we do."

"Maybe, but DelTex needs something else more."

Brooke's eyebrows knit together. "He's downstream from you. I still don't get it."

Gunner motioned for everyone to sit down

at the table. "The way the law works, the government can claim a certain amount of land on either side of any body of 'navigable water'—even a little creek—in the name of drainage, water rights or anything they declare is in the interests of the public good. The bigger the body of water, the more land can be taken. The creek's been especially big this year, and now we know why."

Gran sat up straight. "He's damming up the creek so that our banks are larger. Why? It doesn't help Larkey. It hurts him."

"There's only one reason Larkey would intentionally hinder his own water supply," Gunner continued. "DelTex has to be paying him off."

Brooke frowned. "This already smells like collusion between the state and DelTex, but if they're also playing one rancher off another…"

"Doesn't Larkey realize he's next? Once they swallow us, they'll turn on Larkey." Gran turned to Brooke. "Sorry, dear, but if you didn't know it before, you know now. You work for swine."

Gunner thought that was putting it a bit harshly, but then again, he'd already called Markham and his cohorts far harsher words out by the fence posts.

"We have to get this out, and fast," Gunner advised. "Rostam said the state documents would show up by Friday, didn't he?"

"That's what he said," Gran replied. "I'd better get Ash on the phone tonight."

"Ash?" Brooke asked.

"Ashton Palmer, our family lawyer," Gunner explained. "We'd planned on calling him when the papers came, but I don't think we can wait that long.

Brooke gave Gunner a determined look. "If you call your lawyer—and you should call him—you might win. But if you call a reporter, you *will* win."

"Take this public?" Gunner hadn't expected Brooke to suggest that.

"That's exactly what I'm saying. DelTex

knows they run the risk of looking like a bully with politicians in their pocket when they do something like eminent domain. After all, it's supposed to be a government policy, not something twisted to benefit a private scheme. If it got out that they've done what we think they've done, it's not only alleged corruption, it could create a public backlash strong enough to kill the whole project. Plus, it's an election year in the fall. No politician would want to look like Del-Tex's puppet so close to an election—it'd be good for their image to side with us, even if they've helped DelTex in the past. Maybe especially if they've helped DelTex." She took a deep breath. "You can fight this in the press. Community relations is what I do. I know who to call."

"You'd stick your neck out for us?" Regret began to uncurl in his stomach for all his suspicions about Brooke. She'd be committing professional suicide if she went public against DelTex.

"You ready to burn that bridge?" Gran asked, evidently coming to the same conclusion. "There'd be no going back if you did this. They might not know right away that you are responsible, but they'll know soon enough."

Brooke looked a little shaky, and rightly so. "What they're doing is wrong. I can't stand here and let it happen if I might have a way to stop it."

Gunner looked at her, taking in the unsteady confidence in her eyes, the mixture of nerves and determination that both grounded her and made her fidgety at the same time. It struck him that she was braver than he in many ways. He'd come back to the Blue Thorn when Gran begged, but he'd never made such an unforced choice, such a voluntary, costly stand as Brooke was making right now.

He could believe her, believe *in* her. She may have stepped onto the Blue Thorn with mixed motives way back, but now she was on his side. For a man who'd spent the better part of his life feeling folks line up against him, to know this woman stood beside him changed everything. He felt the shift in his chest, in his world, in his heart. "You sure?" he said, holding her gaze.

"I need to do this. I can't not do this. I know I'll lose my job. Only, what will I have lost, really? I don't think I can work at Del-Tex anymore. Not after what I've seen." She looked up at Gunner, and everything he'd felt for her back at the gala surged up again, sending the hurt and anger into thin air. "I can't work for someone who would do this to you."

Gunner swallowed hard before he said, "Okay. Where do we start?"

"I've got my laptop in the car." Her face grew pink. She'd declared more than her professional integrity today, and they both knew it. Yes, Brooke was lending her hand to the fight to save Blue Thorn, but she was opening her heart to him.

He realized, as he followed Brooke to the car to fetch her briefcase, that he didn't have to extend his heart to her—it was already hers.

"I owe you an apology," he said as she shut her car door, clutching her briefcase to her chest in a way that reminded him of the nervous way Audie clutched her backpack on that first visit. *She's so much stronger than I ever gave her credit for.*

"No, you don't," she said. "You had every right to think I wasn't straight with you."

"I should have believed you. You've been honest with me all along, but I wouldn't see it." He took the briefcase from her, taking her hand instead. "I'm worried for you."

"I'm worried for me, too. And Audie. Markham can be a powerful enemy."

The urge to keep her safe welled up with such force, Gunner felt it like a physical sensation. A surge of adrenaline that made him want to wrap his arms around her and tell the world to back off. As it was, he squeezed her hand. "We know how to deal with predators around here, don't you worry. This herd protects its own." He didn't come right out and say "you're one of us now," but he could see in her eyes that he didn't need to. She knew.

"We need to see the dam with our own eyes," she said as they started walking back to the house. "Take photos if we can. If by some chance that blur is hiding something else, or hiding nothing at all, we've got to know."

"You and I both know that's not the case," Gunner said, "but I think you're right. Only, how?" As Gunner looked toward the barn, he got an idea. "I'll get Billy to bring Audie back to Gran. We'll need him with us. Daisy started this—I think we can get her to end it."

Chapter Seventeen

It was a risky plan. It also meant bringing Brooke into that risk, and that set a cold spot in the pit of Gunner's stomach. Still, they needed that proof now, and he didn't have another option.

"Do you think Daisy and Russet will head over there?" Brooke asked. Gunner had concocted a plan whereby Billy would lead Daisy and Russet to the northwest gate and "happen" to leave it unlatched. Given Daisy's recent hankering to wander, she would cross the road with Russet onto Larkey's land by the gate just a few yards from their own—Gunner was pretty sure she was heading toward it that day she blocked Brooke's path. For a man who pitched a fit when he found animals on his land, Larkey was lazy about locking his gates—which suited Gunner's plan perfectly.

The "lost" animals would provide Gunner and Brooke with an excuse to venture onto Larkey's land in search of the bison. That gate wasn't far from where the suspected dam could be found and documented. Hopefully, they would be in and out with Daisy and Russet before Larkey even knew they were there.

"It's the best chance we've got," Gunner replied, hoping he sounded more confident than he felt. While half of him hated putting Brooke anywhere near Larkey's crosshairs, there was another half that needed Brooke beside him for this. A few months ago, he'd have considered that a weakness—the head of Blue Thorn ought to be able to defend it all on his own. Gran's words kept coming back to him—the ones about being stronger together than they were apart. *Maybe a better man*, he thought as he led Brooke toward the horse barn, *knows when to keep the better woman by his side*.

He glanced at Brooke's eyes as they entered the horse barn. There was fear, but there was the same determination he felt settling down his own spine. They were stronger together. He saw the "it's worth it" conviction in her features that set his own jaw. Maybe that was the place where courage came from.

Acting on a quick impulse, he pulled Brooke off toward the tack room instead of going straight to the horses Billy had saddled. Inside, he opened a drawer in the cabinets that lined the wall. Gunner pulled out a turquoise bandanna and held it up. "Here."

She looked up at him, not understanding the gesture. "What's this?"

"Everyone on the ranch carries one of these." He put it in her hands, feeling some part of his life slide into place as he did. "You're one of us now."

Her eyes widened as that sweet smile— the one that had hooked him back on the muddy road—spread across her face. She knew what it meant and why he'd given it to her now. A surprisingly large part of him wanted to kiss her—right here, right now— but it seemed like the wrong time. Hopefully, the bandanna would speak his intentions for now, and he'd save a good long kiss for after this whole thing was over.

Brooke took the blue square, smiling as she tied it around her neck. Gunner had to admit, the color did wonders for her eyes. She belonged here. Why had it taken this whole mess to force him to figure that out?

"I'm glad you can ride," Gunner said, needing something practical to talk about given the tumbling, falling sensation filling his chest. "We usually herd the bison with ATVs, but they'd be too loud—they'd draw Larkey's attention, for sure."

She tightened the knot on the bandanna with a firm hand. "I can do this. I want to do this."

Gunner took her hand and they walked together toward the horses. Again, he was struck by how she fit into the place—something he never would have guessed given how they'd met. He stopped her one more time before they were ready to mount. "You're sure, now? This could get ugly. If Larkey catches us, he won't be nice."

She nodded. Gunner cupped his hands to give her a boost up onto the horse, but she stopped him, holding hands instead. "Hang on a minute," she said. "There's something I—we need to do first."

"What's that?"

"Pray."

He hadn't expected that. Then again, knowing how Brooke saw the world, knowing what they were about to attempt, it made a surprising sort of sense. He closed his hands around hers, feeling another part of his life slide into place when he did. "Okay," he said softly. He meant it, too.

Brooke closed her eyes, but Gunner found he could not. Instead he watched her, let the moment seep into him despite the unfamiliar feelings. More than just Brooke, he seemed to take in everything about the moment— the movement of the horses, the tender feel of Brooke's hands in his, the slanting sun shining down on a day that would change everything for not only him, but her, too. "Father," she began, "protect us." Her voice was low and peaceful—what faith ought to sound like, even in a jam like this. "See justice done today. If there's a way around this battle, show it to us."

Gunner surprised himself by nodding in agreement. It struck him again just what a wonder of a woman held his hands right now. "Thank You for the way You've provided," she went on, "for this land, these animals, these people. Keep Daisy and Russet safe, and keep us safe, as well. Let the truth come to light without anyone coming to harm." Gunner realized she had named the urge filling him. She'd given the perfect words to his feelings—her gift, she always said, and what a gift that was. "In Your son's name, Amen."

"Amen," he said after her, and it didn't feel odd or forced at all. When Brooke opened her eyes to look at him, the warmth there nearly took Gunner's breath away. "Thanks for that," he managed, his voice catching. She squeezed her fingers where they intertwined with his, and the choice was made. "There's something else we have to do."

"What's that?"

"This." With that he leaned over and kissed her. A warm, slow kiss that was both declaration and promise. A steady, solid kiss that felt very much like the first of many. And everything slid into place.

He ran one hand down her cheek as he pulled back, taking a moment's satisfaction in the color that rose there. It was a fine thing to kiss a woman well, but this was so much more than a very good kiss. Her eyes sparkled—she'd felt it, too. "I was gonna wait, but I changed my mind. Can you blame me?" He slid his hand around her, reveling in the sensation of her in his embrace. "If I'm gonna get shot for trespassing in an hour, I didn't want to go without a first kiss."

"Don't you dare get shot," she replied with an alarmed smirk and placed a hand on his chest. "I'd really hate that to be our last."

"Not on my watch." With that, Gunner hoisted her high enough to slide into the saddle. "You stay well behind me when we meet up with Daisy," he called as he handed her the reins before swinging up onto his own mount. "Bison can jump higher than you'd think, and they can turn on a dime. I can't lasso her like a cow—we've just got to herd her and Russet back across the road."

He took one last, long look as they walked the horses out into the sunlight. "Ready?"

*   *   *

"Ready."

Brooke was surprised to feel the solid core of certainty Jim had always talked about. The part she most admired about him—but the part that cost him everything. She realized, as their horses picked up the pace, that a tiny part of her had resented Jim's stand. After all, his convictions had taken him from her.

Today the resentment was gone. Now, about to take a stand of her own, she understood why Jim's convictions would have never allowed any other choice. She could no more turn back now than Jim could have allowed the theft of that medicine to go unchallenged. Yes, the threat was very real, but so was the peace of knowing she was doing the right thing. Just the day before, she'd questioned the idea that God placed her here to find a solution, but now Brooke knew that was exactly what had happened. She really was ready.

She was also ready to open her heart again. *I'm taking a stand for much more than bison and land,* she thought as they turned toward the northwest gate.

Riding now at full speed behind Gunner, the wind whipping across the rolling green land, Brooke took in the amazing moment. She was heading off on horseback to catch a crook and herd bison. If it wasn't such a treacherous mission, the whole thing would feel like a Wild West adventure. "What if we find her before we see the dam?" she called as she caught up to Gunner.

"That'll complicate things," he called back. "Let's just hope that doesn't happen."

They rode for another ten minutes, the land stretching out wide under a bright sky. Brooke felt the sense of awe she'd always felt about this land rise up, despite her nerves. To her right, she saw the herd out grazing in pastures. Once ranchers and even the Indian nations had seen bison herds that numbered in the tens of thousands. As impressive as Gunner's herd was, what must it have been like to see a herd ten, even fifty times the size of Blue Thorn's thunder across the grass?

She should have been more afraid. She was about to set in motion a series of events that would end her job at DelTex and make some powerful enemies. Brooke felt tension, caution even, but not fear. The solid protection of Gunner Buckton seemed to live in the blue bandanna circling her throat. More than that, God's will seemed to rise up around her, confirming her earlier realization. She *had* been led here for this reason.

Billy was on his way back in from the gate. "She went over, just like we planned. I followed on foot to nudge her and Russet across the creek so she'd be on the far side, but I didn't go as far as the dam." He pointed to the rise of a small hill just across the road from where they stood now. "If she's heading for that crop of trees like I think she is, she ought to be there by now."

"Okay, so it's working so far," Gunner said. "Get on back, Billy, and be ready when we bring Daisy and Russet back home. Don't tell Gran—not yet. I don't want her to worry in front of Audie." He wheeled his horse around as Billy headed back toward the house. Gunner pointed down the road, sending Brooke's gaze over the small bridge that spanned the creek. "There's Larkey's gate down a ways, across the creek. We'll come at it from the other side, to make sure we meet up with Daisy and Russet afterward." They both hesitated as they came to the Blue Thorn gate. There was no going back after this. He looked at her, a silent "here we go" in his eyes.

She nodded. *Father, give me courage. Keep us from harm.*

They cantered down the road where her little blue car had been stopped, muddy gullies still lining the pavement. The metal gate just beyond the little creek bridge was already open, and they walked their horses through it—Gunner first, then Brooke.

It felt treacherous to wind their way down the swollen creek bed. Knowing she was on Larkey's land, Brooke felt exposed and at risk. A half mile in, they found what they were looking for: a collection of cinder blocks, soil and sandbags formed a hasty but sturdy dam.

Gunner let out a low whistle while Brooke reached inside her bag for her digital camera. "I half hoped he hadn't done it," he said, looking down at the structure and the muddy ground it created. "The political stuff I can believe, but this is rancher against rancher. I know my dad and he weren't the best of friends, but this…"

"This is wrong," Brooke said as she snapped several shots of the dam, making sure the time and location stamps were live on her camera. "This isn't public good, Gunner, this is private greed."

"How do you think he ever hoped to get away with it?" Gunner asked.

"I'd guess that this would only stay in place

until DelTex broke ground, or even just got all the permitting clearances. The legislation DelTex was manipulating would do most of the dirty work anyway. They didn't need a permanent dam—they only had to get away with it for a little while."

"Then Larkey could just dismantle the dam, and it wouldn't matter that our creek would go back to its old size."

Brooke moved to get a good angle of the far side of the dam, now not much more than a dry bed. "Just one or two more shots."

"Okay, let's make this quick. I don't want to be out here one second longer than we have to be. It's just enough…"

A yell and a gunshot cracked through the air, startling Brooke so that but for the wrist strap, she might have dropped the camera. *Oh, no.*

"Larkey." Gunner spurred his horse into action, splashing through the swollen creek. "He found them first. Stay here!"

Chapter Eighteen

Gunner dug his heels into the horse's flanks, racing toward the sound of the shot but taking crucial seconds to veer his horse as far from the creek as possible. If Larkey knew he'd seen the dam, there was no telling what the man would do. He was clearly comfortable firing a gun at Gunner's stock already. Daisy's bellow—and it had to be Daisy, because Larkey raised cattle, not bison—confirmed his worst fears. He knew he was taking a chance here—Larkey had often threatened Gunner's animals with harm if they had ever wandered onto his land. It was what had made the issue of Daisy's wandering tendencies and the faulty northwest gate so troubling.

But more than just bison were in danger. Would Brooke remember to stay back if Daisy and Russet were panicked and ran toward the creek? Daisy had a temper if threatened, and if Larkey had done anything to threaten her calf, she'd show that temper in spades.

Don't let Larkey have shot them. Gunner was surprised to find the wish took the form of a prayer, remembering how Brooke had prayed for their protection as they fought for justice. Maybe Daisy and Russet were okay. If Larkey's gunfire had only been a warning shot, Gunner thought he might be able to talk himself out of the jam.

If his diversionary detour hadn't worked, however, if Larkey worked out where he and Brooke had been and why…well, he was going to need a lot more prayer to come out of this unharmed.

Coming up over the hill, Gunner let out a growl of anger as he saw Paul Larkey and three of his hands standing in ATVs with rifles pointed at Daisy and Russet.

"Larkey!" he yelled, pulling his horse up when the rancher turned to him—without dropping his weapon.

Stay back, Brooke, he pleaded silently. *Don't be brave now. Keep down where he can't see you.*

Gunner forced an apologetic tone into his voice, even though he yearned for Daisy to ram the man right off his vehicle. "You found 'em. Good. Daisy's wandering is gonna be the death of me."

Poor choice of words. Lackey raised the rifle so that Gunner was staring down its barrel. "Could be."

"Okay, I get you're steamed. But did you have to shoot at my calf?"

"Didn't hit 'em. Yet. But something's got to teach your beasts to stay off my land."

Russet gave a small snort as if he'd heard

Larkey's warning. Daisy clearly sensed the threat and began pacing and snorting. If Gunner didn't keep every human being well away from that angry mother, she'd show what harm a full-size bison could do.

Keep Larkey talking. "Well, you just riled Daisy up and made the job of getting them back that much harder. She won't play nice now—with either you or me. You might want to back up a couple of yards—she can run fast." Gunner slowly walked his horse up until he was standing between Daisy and Larkey.

"Getting her off my land ain't my problem, it's yours. I told you it'd come to this if I found her—or you—here."

Gunner had a mouthful of things to say about who was causing the problems here, but he swallowed his temper. He had to protect Brooke and the animals, even if it meant drawing Larkey's fire—literally. "I know. And if I had the money to rebuild that gate, it'd be done already. I'm doing the best I can here, Paul, so let's just lower the guns, okay? Neighbors?" The conciliatory words burned in his throat, but he forced a smile to his face anyway.

"You got ten minutes to get those hunks of fur off my property, Buckton."

That gave Gunner an idea. "Well, in that case I'm gonna need some help. Daisy's not going to go nicely now that you shot at her calf. It's going to take at least two of us. You can either wait until Billy gets here or you or one of your men can give me a hand." Gunner hoped Brooke wasn't behind him. If she came up over the hill to help, he'd have a hard time explaining her presence away.

"I don't think I'm of any mind to lend you anything," Larkey said. "Maybe I'll just fire my rifle again or gun the ATV engine to scare her off."

"Don't!" Gunner shouted. That would be the worst thing to do. "You rile her more and she'll likely charge us all. I'd like to keep my ribs right where they are, if you don't mind."

"Nine minutes, then."

Russet gave another bellow. Nine minutes wasn't enough time to get Billy over here—he'd be all the way back to the barn by now. If he called Brooke up from behind him to help, he'd place both of them in further danger. Right now the only way out was to try to coax Daisy and Russet back on his own—a nearly impossible task in the short time frame Larkey was allowing. *If You'd like to make good on Brooke's prayer, Lord, now would be the right time.*

Dismissing his father's advice to "never turn your back on an armed and angry man," Gunner turned his horse to face Daisy and her calf. Sensing the bison's mood, Gunner's horse balked. "Easy, fella. We got this. Just go slow." Gunner moved two feet toward the animals. "Hee-ya!" he called as loudly as he dared, waving his blue bandanna. "Get on back to the Blue Thorn, Daisy." He angled his position so that he placed Daisy between himself and Larkey's gate.

Russet took two or three steps in the right direction. "Good boy, Russet. Go on, mama, take your baby home."

Daisy turned her head to glare at Gunner. *I'm sorry I got you into this, girl*, Gunner pleaded silently. *Just help me out here and we'll be okay.*

His cell phone went off in his pocket, and while his first thought was to ignore it, the realization that it could be Brooke made him reach for the device.

It was a text from Billy.

Brooke safe. On my way.

He wasn't sure how Brooke had managed it, but he shot a gush of thanks heavenward and turned to Larkey. "Billy heard the shots and is on the way. We'll have our bison out of here in ten minutes."

Larkey's response was to hike his rifle up on his shoulder. "Excepting you only got eight."

He had to buy time. "Did you hear DelTex

has somehow whipped up the legislation to take my creek? Eminent domain. Once all that legal mumbo jumbo is in place, don't you worry that you'll be next?"

Lackey did not reply, but neither did he look completely surprised. How much did the rancher know?

"They're gonna eat me alive, Larkey, and only a fool would think they'll stop with me."

Lackey snorted. "Quit your yapping and get those animals out of here."

"I'm trying." Gunner moved his horse closer to Daisy and was rewarded with her turning away from him to face Larkey's gate. Good. That was progress. *Come on, girl, get out of here and do us both a favor.* "They've got the politicians in their back pocket, Larkey. It won't stop with my creek," Gunner called as he circled his horse. "You know what happens when eminent domain kicks in. They pay us next to nothing and come up with reasons to take more. You'll be next, Larkey, and you know it."

Evidently, he'd pushed an inch too far, for Larkey raised the rifle in his direction. "I said git."

Gunner was just about to risk heading toward Daisy on his own when he saw Billy come riding up to the Blue Thorn gate. "Look at that—Billy made it here in time." He tipped his hat at Larkey, frustration tumbling with relief in his gut. "We'll be outta your hair in no time. Sorry for your trouble."

It took fourteen minutes for Billy and Gunner to get Daisy and Russet off Larkey's land and back behind the gate that closed them onto the Blue Thorn. Good thing Larkey stopped counting.

Brooke paced outside the barn, scanning the horizon every ten seconds. She didn't know how many gunshots she'd heard, and her brain was concocting dozens of deadly scenarios. Why was it taking so long? For all she knew, Larkey could have ordered Gunner arrested for trespassing.

It had taken every ounce of self-control she had not to ride up that hill behind Gunner. Once she'd worked out that she could dismount and follow the creek bed under the bridge that spanned the road, sidestepping the fencing that had been pulled down by the swollen current, Brooke had ridden for the barn and Billy as fast as she could.

Please, Lord. Let them come home safe. All of them. Now that there was even the slimmest chance they could save Blue Thorn Ranch from DelTex and their legislative cronies, Brooke couldn't bear the thought that they'd fail. Her grief that this had all been her fault was as powerful as it was irrational. She had no leverage over anything DelTex did. The fact was that if she hadn't even tried to find a compromise, DelTex would probably have defaulted to eminent domain even faster than they had. This wasn't her fault.

But the drumming, overwhelming need to make it right? That was all her.

And all Gunner. Her fascination with the Blue Thorn was only partly due to the beauty of the land and its animals. The connection she felt—the connection she could no longer cut—was to Gunner. To the way he was part of the land, the courage he'd shown to swallow his rebellious pride and come home to keep the ranch alive. To the wave of feelings that raced through her when he kissed her. His fierce sense of protectiveness and purpose struck a deep chord in her. She was so tired of struggling to make it alone, so weary of spending her days selling pretty houses. She wanted to be part of this, part of something real—part of Gunner's life.

Audie did, too. She came alive on the ranch in ways Brooke had never seen. Jim's death had hit Audie hard. No one that age should be shouldering a lost parent. Audie's connection to little Russet filled a need, made something settle for her that Brooke couldn't explain but still knew to be essential.

And Adele. What an extraordinary woman. Adele could teach her so much about life and strength and family. Yes, she loved her own parents, and always would, but life would be so much richer for Adele's presence.

I love him. I love all of them. I love this place. Please, Lord, please. I don't believe You led me here just to watch it all go away.

Brooke continued to pray, thankful Adele had taken it upon herself to distract Audie in the kitchen with making cookies. How could that woman stay so calm and collected while her grandson risked his life to save their land? *She has twice the faith in You I have*, Brooke prayed, feeling as if she was going to pace a ditch into the ground in front of the barn. *She has so much to teach me. To teach Audie.*

"Hee-ya, girl!"

Brooke practically fell against the barn in relief as she heard Gunner's voice and saw the figures of two bison and two horses come down over the hill. They were moving very slowly, Gunner and Billy circling around the pair of animals.

She heard the screen door bang open behind her and turned to see Adele and Audie on the porch.

"They're back!" Audie yelled and started running for the pastures.

"Hold on." Brooke caught Audie's arm, remembering Gunner's cautions about the danger of approaching threatened animals. If Larkey's gunshot had spooked them, caution was needed. "We need to let Gunner and Billy bring them in first."

Brooke's heart wanted her to run up the pasture hill with Audie's abandon, but she held back. Gunner looked unharmed as he and Billy slowly guided Daisy and Russet into the holding pen. The minute the animals were contained, he came over the fence and pulled Brooke into his arms.

"You clever woman," he said into her hair,

tightening his grip. "You smart, brave, beautiful thing." He kissed the top of her hair, making Audie whoop in surprise and giggle.

The noise pulled Gunner down to hunch eye to eye with Audie. "Your mama is the smartest thing I've ever seen. You are, too."

"Are Russet and Daisy okay?"

Brooke loved how Gunner took Audie's questions seriously. "I think so. Right now, they're scared and annoyed, but they'll settle down in time. If I think he's hurt in any way, I'll check with the vet, 'cause you and I both know how special he is."

Russet's not the only one who's special, Brooke thought. If the way Gunner looked at her wasn't already enough to win her heart, the way Gunner looked at Audie sealed the deal.

"Hey, Audie, all this drama has me starved. Did I hear Billy say you made cookies with Gran?"

Audie grinned. "Oatmeal chocolate chip."

"How did you know those were my absolute favorite? Can you go tell Gran to get some ready and help her out? We need to leave Daisy and Russet alone to calm down anyway."

Audie looked longingly toward the pen before consenting. "Okay."

As Gunner straightened up while Audie made for the door, Brooke took his face in her hands and kissed him again.

"Wow." A satisfying delirium washed over Gunner's features for a moment. "Today has certainly improved."

"Did Larkey really shoot at Russet? Is that legal?"

Gunner's face darkened. "Legal? Yes. Right? No. Kinda like what DelTex is trying to pull, if you ask me."

Brooke tightened her hold on Gunner. "I was terrified he'd shoot you."

"I'd like to think he wouldn't stoop to murder. Not that our friend Larkey seems to put much stock in laws." He kissed Brooke's forehead, and she felt it tingle all the way to her toes. "I'm okay. And so are you. How'd you ever think to go under the road and fetch Billy?"

"I didn't at first. My brain went blank for a minute or two. Only, I knew I had to do something, even if it was just getting out of there the way I knew you'd want me to. So I prayed hard and fast for an idea, and that's when I saw that the fence under the bridge was knocked down by the water flow."

"I'm starting to grow fond of those prayers of yours." Gunner stared into her eyes, and Brooke felt as if the whole sky had swallowed her in happiness. "I'm sorry I ever doubted you. I was so hurt and angry because...well, because I'd fallen for you. Hard. And today, just a little bit harder." He ran his hand through her hair. "Don't go back to DelTex. I don't want you anywhere near that snake Markham. I want you here, beside me, fighting for the Blue Thorn."

Brooke hadn't even realized how much she

wanted to hear those words until Gunner spoke them. "What if we don't win?"

"We will. Even if not this battle, then the next one. I love you, Brooke. I need you here. I know it's messy and we have to work a lot of things out but I think—"

Brooke silenced him with a kiss. "I don't think, I know. Yes. We'll stay."

Gunner pulled his hat off his head. "Wait… did I just ask you to marry me?"

She smiled. "Well, I am the communications expert here, so I'd say yes."

"And you did—say yes, I mean—didn't you?" Gunner's arms slid around her waist.

"Uh-huh."

He rewarded her with a heart-stopping kiss. "Should I ask Audie if it's okay with her?"

"I love that you think of her. I love you. She loves you, too."

"Gran's gonna go crazy when I tell her."

Gunner took her hand and walked toward the house. "Today just keeps getting better and better."

Chapter Nineteen

"Really?" Audie's eyes were as big as saucers.

"Really," Gunner replied, feeling his grin widen. "If it's okay with you."

Her response was to fling herself at him with such a joyful burst that it knocked him over. "Yes! You sure can marry Mama!"

"I can't believe it," Gran said from the couch, where she was hugging Brooke. "When I prayed and prayed God would make something good out of this whole mess, I hadn't counted on this much good." Gran was wiping tears from her eyes, and

Brooke didn't look as if her own tears were far behind.

"Hey, not so much crying over there. This is happy stuff," Gunner teased.

"Big happy stuff," Audie amended. "A dozen cookies happy stuff."

"Well…" started Brooke.

She was cut off by Billy, who came through the door to stare amazed at Gunner and Audie sprawled on the floor while Gran and Brooke sat on the couch wiping tears. "Daisy's calming down fine. What's going on?"

"We're getting married!" Audie exclaimed.

Gunner drew a breath to correct Audie, then stopped himself. It was true, in a sense, wasn't it? He decided the best response was to grin at Billy. If anyone had told him he'd be grinning like this today, he'd never have believed it. Everything was still a mess, he was still in the fight of his life for his family's ranch, but somehow he'd gained a rock-solid hope that everything would work out all right in the end. That changed everything.

"You don't say?" Billy said, crossing his arms over his chest. "Wasn't expecting that."

"Neither was I," Gran said.

"Me, neither!" Audie called. "Can I see Russet now?"

Gunner sat up and settled Audie onto his lap. She fit perfectly, something that made his heart flip over in his chest. "You're still gonna have to wait. But we do have some cookies to pass the time, and your mama and I have a whole bunch of emails and faxes to send."

"Work?" Audie frowned at Brooke. "Today?"

Brooke rose from the couch. "Very important work. After all, the Blue Thorn means even more to us now, doesn't it?"

Gunner watched Audie connect the facts—it was fun to see the idea light up her sweet face. "I'm gonna live here?"

"That's the idea. So don't worry about

Russet—you'll be seeing a lot of him from here on in."

Audie's grin just about melted Gunner's heart. Whatever came from the stand they took today, he knew he'd fight with everything he had to save the Blue Thorn. The people in this room were as much his family as his brother and sisters scattered across the country. The Blue Thorn was the hub that held them all together. It was the place he wanted to build the rest of his life, now that he knew who that life included.

He could never have predicted or planned the wild chain of events that had happened since he came across that little blue car outside his fence. And yet, looking back, everything seemed to line up in a perfect order toward the current moment. He knew what Gran would say about that. He knew what Brooke would say about that, too. And, for the first time in a long time, he believed it. God really could take any situation and turn it for good. God had watched over him, bringing just the right people into his life at just the right time. His faith—something he thought long abandoned—pushed up through the dry earth of his rebellion to spring new and green like the grass did every year on the pastures. *Thanks for holding on*, he prayed silently, feeling a deep, transforming gratitude. *Sorry it took so long.*

He needed a ten-hour conversation with Brooke, but that wasn't possible. At least not until they showed the world what they'd found in Larkey's creek. The task was daunting, but Gunner felt stronger than he had in years. He realized now that it was Gran's faith and Grandpa's love that gave her the amazing resilience he so admired. It used to bug him how Gran's response to any crisis was "God's got it covered." For the first time, Gunner felt as if he believed it, as well.

He looked up at Brooke, a thousand things passing between them in the quiet way he held her eyes, before he lifted Audie to her feet and stood himself. "Ready?"

"Ready," she said.

For the next two hours, Gunner and Brooke downloaded photos, crafted emails, scanned Brooke's press contact list, reviewed government watchdog web pages and even raided Gran's address book in order to tell everyone who would listen what they suspected DelTex had done.

"I should be terrified," Brooke said as she rolled her shoulders while watching yet another fax inch its way through the machine. "But I'm not. I feel like...well, like I've been on the wrong road for a long time and finally found the right one. Does that make any sense?"

Gunner came up behind her and rubbed her shoulders. It felt right—grounding and yet exhilarating at the same time—to be working alongside her. "I get it. My heart's thumping in six different ways for twelve different reasons, but I'm not scared."

Brooke turned to look at him, her eyes radiant. He could envision seeing that same expression fifty years from now and never tiring of it. For a man who'd made a life of bumping from one thing to the next, that was a startling notion. "Heart-thumping?" she quoted. "Who knew you had a way with words? I thought that was my job."

She turned to tuck herself into his arms while the fax machine churned its way through the pages, and sure enough, his heart thumped harder. "And you? Coming up with a plan to gallop off and save the day? I thought that was my job."

Brooke laid her head on his chest, and an extraordinary peace wound its way around Gunner's heart despite the chaos surrounding him. "If anyone had told me I could be so happy in the midst of such a mess, I'd have laughed in their face." He kissed the top of her head. "Thank you."

That turned her face up to his. "Don't thank me yet. The legislation may already be in place. We don't know if any of this will work. The only outcome of all of this

could still be my getting fired when I con-
front Markham with what I've found."

"Don't you go back there. Not even for an
hour."

"Don't you think I need to accuse him
face-to-face?"

"He hasn't earned the right to anything
from you. I'll go with you if you feel you
have to do that, but I'll tell you right now—I
can't stand the thought of Markham anywhere near you."

"Well, then, I guess we have one more fax
to send. My resignation."

Gunner felt a little shudder go through her
at the word. It struck him again just how
much Brooke was putting on the line here,
and it made him love her all the more for it.
He tightened his arms around her. "Don't
you worry. You carry a blue bandanna now.
That means you're under my protection, and
I will never let anything happen to you and
Audie. God's got this."

Her eyes glistened at his words even as her

shoulders softened in his embrace. "He does, doesn't He?" Everything had changed, him most of all. The bristling, keep-the-world-at-a-distance part of him—the part he'd long considered his strength—wasn't a strength at all. It was a wall, a false armor that hadn't protected as he thought, but had smothered him instead. Now that it was gone, it felt as if his breath pulled in a whole new kind of air, silly as that sounded.

A small, light laugh bubbled up from her, and he reveled in the feel of it against his chest. "Is my faith that amusing?" he asked.

Brooke reached up to cup his cheek with one hand. "Not at all. I was just wondering if Daisy knew what she was doing."

Gunner laughed as well, remembering the very odd look Daisy had given him as she squared off against Brooke's car that afternoon. "Could be."

Her eyes closed. "Thank You, Lord." She opened them again. "Thank you, Daisy. Thank you, Gunner Buckton Junior."

He felt a grin crinkle the corners of his eyes. "Brooke Buckton. Think it has too many *B*'s?"

"Nope," she said, leaning up to kiss his cheek. "It's perfect."

The next two days went by in a blur of phone calls, documents, phone conversations and surprising pockets of calm. Brooke stood among the sea of boxes in her kitchen Friday morning and considered her circumstances. She'd thought she would feel as though she'd jumped off a cliff—one long, scary fall—but she didn't. What she had said to Gunner was right: it felt like walking into a clearing or like finding the right road after having been lost. Easy? No, exposing DelTex had been one of the hardest things she had ever done.

Still, they'd succeeded. An Austin newspaper had jumped on the story within hours, and their investigation had cast DelTex's actions and even some of the involved politicians in sufficient bad light that the Ramble

Acres project had been effectively stalled until further notice.

Gunner walked into the kitchen with another box. "These go out to the ranch?"

"Yes," she said, crossing another task off the large to-do list taped to the fridge door. "And the other one by the dresser." They'd decided to set up rooms in the Blue Thorn guesthouse for her and Audie so they could spend weekends there. With a house to sell and two months of school still to go, it was best not to make Audie shift to a school district out by the ranch until next year. The commute didn't feel like too much of a sacrifice to spend more time with the family she had come to love. Besides, not fleeing her house here made a sort of stand for Brooke. An "I'm not hiding from you" declaration that while DelTex was huge, they couldn't make her turn tail and run.

Not that she didn't treasure every moment with Gunner. He'd shown such a tender, protective side since that day on Larkey's ranch. As he opened up to her, she found new things to love about him. *There was a part of me frightened I would never love again*, she thought as she watched Gunner haul the box of Audie's stuffed animals—not the stuffed bison, for that stayed wherever Audie was—to his truck. *But now I feel as if I love even more.* Somehow, she knew Jim would bless her new life. He'd want Audie to have a father figure as she grew up, and he'd never want Brooke to go through life alone.

She felt Gunner's hands slip around her waist as she stood staring out her kitchen window. "Where were you? You looked a million miles away just now."

She turned to him. "Thinking about how I wasn't sure today would ever happen." It was a poor explanation, but she couldn't quite put her feelings into words despite her professional credentials.

"Moving partly out to the ranch?"

"No." Brooke sighed. She owed him an explanation. "It's just...well...there was a part of me that wondered if I'd ever be happy again. After..."

Gunner kissed her forehead. "It's okay to say his name. I can share you with Jim's memory. He's Audie's father. And I endorse his taste in brides."

How did that man always know the exact right thing to say? "I'm so thankful you'll be a huge part of Audie's life. You'll be as much her father as Jim, you know. Even more so in some ways."

"I know," Gunner said, smiling as if it was the best job a man could have, "and I'm glad. But about that bride part..." He stepped away from her, reaching into his pocket to produce a small blue velvet pouch. Brooke caught her breath as he got down on one knee.

A beautiful ring with a center diamond and sparkling light blue stones on either side spilled from the pouch onto his palm. "This was my mother's, and Gran's before her. This ring belongs to the women of Blue Thorn. And now it belongs to you. Brooke

Calder, will you be my wife? Asked right and proper this time, mind you."

The house was a mess. No one really knew yet if DelTex had been permanently stopped from their attempts to grab Blue Thorn land. They still hadn't figured out where Audie would go to school next year or how and when they would sell this house.

None of that mattered in the face of the man on his knee before her. There was only one answer to give—the one she'd already given. "Yes."

Gunner slipped the jewel onto her finger, kissing the back of her hand once he did. Then he stood and gave her a long, lingering kiss that made her forget every single unresolved detail of her current chaos.

"If it's okay with you," Gunner said as he kissed each of the fingertips on her left hand, "it'll be Audie's one day, too. Unless you and I have a son someday—then he gets to pick the hand who wears it."

Children with Gunner. The prospect set

off a bank of fireworks in Brooke's chest. So much of life was opening up before her. "Gunner Buckton the third?"

"Only if you say so."

"Audie'd go nuts to have a baby brother." Brooke felt as if the entire house couldn't hold the size of her happiness. Maybe not even all of the Blue Thorn. "She's crazy enough about Russet as it is." The ranch had seen two more calves born since Russet, and Audie had picked excellent names for each one—without a single Rainbow Sparkle in sight.

"We'll let God work out the timing on that. The wedding will be enough on our plates while all this land nonsense works itself out." The Special Entity eminent domain legislation Senator Rostam had warned Adele about had evidently died quietly in committee once the press about DelTex hit. Would it all hold off for good? It was too early to tell. "Are you going to want a big to-do? My sister Ellie's getting all serious with her guy in Atlanta, and I've a mind to beat her to the altar." He looked as if he'd stomach a large event if she wanted one, but it was clear he didn't cherish the idea. His face reminded her of the way he looked when he tugged on his tux shirt collar—cooperating but far from comfortable.

"Not that I don't love the way you look in a tux," she teased, "but I think a small ceremony out on the ranch ought to do just fine. My folks will come in from Oklahoma, I'm sure. And I've already got my little maid of honor, don't I?"

Gunner's eyes popped, as if he'd just remembered something. "If my brother and sisters come, it'll be the first time we've all been together on the ranch in years. You'll love Ellie. I told her about our engagement last night, and I had to hold the phone away from my ears, she screamed so loud. She's dying to meet you. She's the one who made Audie's stuffed bison."

Brooke settled herself against Gunner's

chest, blissful. "I remember. I'm sure I'll love your family."

Gunner's arms tightened around her, doubling the bliss. "I know I love mine. Welcome to the Blue Thorn, future Mrs. Buckton."

Brooke nodded to the piles of boxes and bags that filled the kitchen around them. "I'm not there yet."

"You are in all the ways that count. As for everything else…"

She knew what he was going to say. She said it with him, a promise they would hold on to together from now on: "God's got it covered."

* * * * *

Dear Reader,

I never planned to spend so much time in Texas. Funny how life takes turns we never expected, isn't it? Suddenly my son was enrolled in the University of Texas, and I kept reading about bison everywhere I looked. That's the joy of being a writer—you can take what life sends your way and make something amazing from a set of coincidences. Only, they aren't coincidences, are they? Brooke and Gunner learn that God will use even the most surprising events to lead us down the path to His healing and purpose.

I hope you'll continue to join me on Blue Thorn Ranch as Gunner and his siblings make their lives on the family land. Look for Gunner's sister Ellie to get her own happy ending in the book *Coming Home to Texas* to be released in May 2016, with twin brother and sister Luke and Tess to follow in the coming months. As always, I love to hear from

you. Email me at allie@alliepleiter.com, visit
my website at www.alliepleiter.com or find
me on Facebook and Twitter.

Blessings,